LOVED BY THE ORC

HIDDEN HOLLOW
BOOK 4

EVANGELINE ANDERSON

Loved by the Orc, 1st Edition,
Copyright © 2025 by Evangeline Anderson
All rights reserved.

This book is a work of fiction. The names, characters, places and incidents are products of the writers' imagination or have been used factiously and are not to be construed as real. Any resemblance to persons, living or dead, actual events, locale or organizations is entirely coincidental.

All rights are reserved. No part of this book may be used or reproduced in any manner whatsoever without written permission except in the case of brief quotations embodied in critical articles and reviews.

This ebook is licensed for your personal enjoyment only. This ebook may not be re-sold or given away to other people. If you would like to share this book with another person, please purchase an additional copy for each person you share it with. If you're reading this book and did not purchase it, or it was not purchased for your use only, then you should return to a retailer of your choice or evangelineanderson.com and purchase your own copy. Thank you for respecting the author's work.

**Cover content is for illustrative purposes only.
Any person depicted on the cover is a model.**

AUTHOR'S NOTES

Very important—please read before you dive into the book!

I'm trying something new with this novella. I personally love Daddy books but I know many of my readers don't. So I decided to write this book with ALL my readers in mind. Here's the deal—when you come to the spicy chapters, there will be a little note at the top letting you know that if you have a Daddy kink and want to read those chapters as Daddy chapters, you can go to the end and find them in the Bonus Daddy Section (Page 119). Then go back to the next regular chapter in the story to continue the book. If you don't have a Daddy kink, just ignore the Bonus Daddy Section. And let me know how this works for you—if you like it, I might do it with more books.

Hugs and Happy Reading,
Evangeline

PROLOGUE
HARMONY

"What's wrong, baby? What happened to make you so upset?" Tark frowned down at me, his bushy black eyebrows pulled low with concern.

"What makes you think I'm upset?" I looked up at him briefly—it was a long way to look. Tark is a full-blooded Orc, which means he's over eight feet tall. I'm human, and tall for a woman, but the top of my head still barely reaches his elbow.

"You're here early, for one thing. And I can always tell by the way you hold your mouth—and how tight your voice sounds," Tark rumbled.

He has this deep, gravely voice that can sound absolutely terrifying when he feels like someone is threatening my safety. But it can also be incredibly soothing when he's being sweet—which he always is with me.

My boyfriend is one big, green flag, and I'm not just saying that because his skin is literally olive green, (even though it is.) He also has tusks curving up from the teeth in his lower jaw and golden eyes that glow in the dark. He looks absolutely terrifying to be honest—I was so scared I fainted the first time I saw him. But the way he's so sweet and kind to me, especially when I'm feeling down, is what drew me to him and it's what I consider to be his defining characteristic.

He was giving me that worried look again and part of me just wanted to melt into his arms. But there was another part—a hard part—that wanted to make it on my own. A part of me that was still afraid to take the comfort I knew he would offer me if I just let my guard down.

"I'm fine," I said, brushing past him and walking into his living room. I always felt like a kid in a fairytale when I spent time in his house—which is located off of Main Street in the magical town of Hidden Hollow.

All the furniture is too big for me—the chairs are so high I have to clamber onto them and so deep that if I sit all the way back my legs dangle like a little girl's. The coffee table comes up to my pelvis and I sink into the carpet up to my ankles—it's extra deep. Also, the fireplace is big enough to roast an entire cow in—not that Tark uses it for that. He's a vegetarian, if you can believe it.

"Babygirl, please—talk to me," he rumbled, coming up behind me and putting one massive hand gently on my shoulder. "Come on, what happened?"

I turned to face him.

"Nothing—I told you."

He frowned and his face was suddenly scary, reminding me that he only showed his sweet side to me.

"Was it that asshole of a human boss again?" he growled and this time his voice had taken on a menacing tone. "Was he bothering you?"

"No," I said, which was a total lie. It absolutely *was* my boss, Mr. Irving Price, the Director of Operations at Bentley Pharmaceuticals and my direct supervisor. He'd belittled me in front of several other people in my department that day and called me "stupid, and fat" which was really hard to swallow.

Naturally, on paper, that kind of thing wasn't allowed at Bentley—at least not according to the HR Department. But in reality, Mr. Price was the CEO's brother and he could pretty much get away with doing or saying whatever he damn well pleased.

In fact, it was thanks to Mr. Price that I'd found my way to Hidden Hollow in the first place. As I stared up at my Orc boyfriend, I couldn't help remembering the very first time I'd ever seen him…

It was just another Tuesday at Bentley Pharmaceuticals…which meant that it was just another day of abuse for me. I was supposed to be an administrative assistant but my position was closer to that of office slave. Though maybe it might be more accurate to say I was my boss's whipping boy. Or girl—you get the idea.

"Miss Ward, come here!"

Just hearing my voice called in that nasty tone made my stomach drop and my heart start thudding unhappily in my chest. I knew I had done something wrong again—or if not, Mr. Price, my boss, would *make up* something that I had done wrong…some rule I'd never heard of that I had broken or some task he'd never actually assigned me had gone undone and now I was in trouble because of it.

"Yes, Mr. Price?" I asked, hurrying into his office.

My boss was sitting in his high-backed chair, rigid as a poker, as he stared down at a pile of papers on his desk. He was a thin man—my grandma would have called him "skinny as a string bean" and he was going bald up top. Because of this, he wore his hair in a classic comb-over with four skinny strands of dark brown hair scraped over the shiny dome of his skull. He had on reading glasses, which were perched on the very tip of his long, bony nose and his watery blue eyes were glaring angrily at me.

"Miss Ward, *what* is this?" he demanded, gesturing to the papers on his desk.

"Er…those are the reports you asked for," I said, wondering what I could have done wrong now. I had stacked them neatly and stapled them in the top middle of each sheet, like he demanded. When I had first started working for him, he'd thrown a fit because I stapled some documents in the top left corner. He demanded that I reprint all of them and "staple them correctly." Ever since, I'd been careful to get that little detail right.

"These reports," he said, glaring at me as he held one out. "The Rainard report is on top. And then right under that, the Connor report."

"Uh…" I shook my head, mystified. "I'm not sure I understand what's wrong."

"*Why* aren't they *alphabetized?*" Mr. Price demanded. "C comes before R in the alphabet—surely even someone as *stupid* as you knows that, Miss. Ward!"

"Alphabetized?" I repeated, shaking my head. "But Mr. Price, you never said—"

"I did! I told you the minute you became my secretary that I wanted all the reports alphabetized!" he shouted, his narrow face going red. He began ripping the pages apart and throwing them on the floor around his desk. "How can you not understand such a simple thing? How *stupid* can you be?"

I felt my face go rigid, turning into a non-threatening, apologetic mask it always becomes when someone shouts at me.

"I…I'm so sorry," I heard myself say. "I'll take them back and alphabetize them right now."

"You're damn right, you will!" He threw the last of the stack of papers on the floor and rose to his feet. "Get down there and pick those up and get them right," he commanded, pointing at the papers—some of which he was currently trampling. "I'm going to my meeting. You'd better have them done when I get back."

And he stalked off, the papers crunching under his shiny, hateful shoes.

Stooping, I began gathering the crumpled paperwork with red cheeks and stinging eyes. I hated myself for making that "sorry face"— for backing down and taking the blame when it wasn't my fault. My boss had *never* told me he wanted anything alphabetized before today, but of course now he was gaslighting me and acting like it was a rule I'd always known about that I had broken.

I had spent a long time getting all the documents just right—now I would have to spend even longer fixing the mess he'd made of them. And I knew without asking that any papers that had been trampled and torn by his feet would need to be reprinted and re-stapled—I didn't dare hand him anything less than a perfect stack of alphabetized reports or he would blow his top again and probably call me "stupid" or an "idiot," or something even worse.

If you're wondering why I put up with this abuse, well—it wasn't by choice. I had signed a contract with Bentley Pharmaceuticals early in my academic career. They had agreed to put me through school and help me become a pharmacist as long as I promised to work for them during school and for two years after. I could take most of my classes online at night and work for them during the day.

It had seemed like a sweetheart deal at the time. I knew people who were drowning in student debt and this way I wouldn't have to take a single loan—well, unless I quit before the contract said I could. At that point, every single dollar that Bentley had loaned to me would suddenly become due—with ten percent interest—in a single lump sum.

Since I didn't have an extra hundred thousand dollars just lying around, I couldn't quit. And my boss, Mr. Price, knew that.

I'd tried to get out from under his thumb several times. But the last time I went to HR, Mrs. Renard, the woman in charge, had asked me bluntly if I just wanted to nullify my contract and pay what I owed the company.

"Of course not!" I exclaimed, feeling all the blood rush from my face when I thought of that much debt suddenly coming down on my head all at once. "I can't afford to pay everything back like that—if I could, I wouldn't have signed the contract in the first place!"

"Then it appears you have no choice but to go back to your

position," Mrs. Renard remarked. She had short, iron-gray hair and a stern face like a disapproving principal.

"But…but it's clear that Mr. Price isn't happy with my performance!" I exclaimed, trying to think of another way to get away from him. "He's always calling me 'stupid' and 'lazy' and 'ignorant' and things like that. Surely he'd rather have someone else as his assistant!"

"I'm afraid not," Mrs. Renard said blandly. "In fact, he's given you nothing but glowing performance reviews. I have a difficult time believing that he calls you 'stupid' when he seems so happy with your work."

It was at that moment I knew that I was trapped. My boss, Irving Price, was never going to let me go. He liked having someone to shout at and abuse. Someone who was too afraid to fight back.

I hadn't even told the HR Director all of the things he called me. The worst was when he talked about my weight and called me "fat" or "chubby." I think those words hurt me most of all because they were true.

I mean, I *knew* I wasn't stupid—I'd graduated top of my class and I had a 4.0 GPA, which isn't easy in Pharmacy School. Have you ever taken Organic Chemistry? It's not exactly a walk in the park—but I aced it.

So I could mostly shrug off his hateful remarks about my IQ. But when it came to my weight, well…that was a number where I was most vulnerable. And I was sure that Mr. Price knew it.

So I was stuck—which was exactly what I was thinking as I sniffed back tears and gathered the torn and trampled documents around my evil boss's desk. Stuck with no way out for at least the next four years!

The worst thing was, the abuse I got from my boss reminded me a lot of the way my uncle and aunt had treated me growing up. My mom died of breast cancer when I was ten and my dad had left before that, when I was only eight. So rather than letting me go into the foster care system, my mom's brother and his wife adopted me.

Sometimes I think it would have been better in foster care. I could never do anything good enough—could never please them. Even my excellent grades didn't make them happy—*nothing* did. It also didn't help that both of them were skinny and I've been chubby all my life. I was just a big disappointment—a burden they had to bear and nothing I could do would ever make them love me or even like me.

That was how I felt with Mr. Price—like I could never make him happy, no matter how hard I tried.

"So why do I keep trying?" I muttered to myself as I gathered the papers. Hot tears splashed on the stack in my hands and I realized I was crying—which would only make my sadistic boss angrier if he came back and saw me "bawling."

Rising to my feet, I shoved the stack of papers to one side of the desk. I needed some time alone—five minutes to get myself together, I thought. I couldn't have a breakdown right here in my boss's office—who knew when he might come back?

I rushed down the hallway, heading for the ladies room. I noticed that the door looked slightly different—were the edges of it glowing? But my eyes were too blurry with tears to make out the details and I just wanted to be alone. I was nearly running as I pushed blindly at the door, which swung open…

And dumped me out in the middle of Hidden Hollow.

1

HARMONY

Hidden Hollow is a magical town located somewhere in the woods of New England. I don't know its exact geographical location—nobody does, I don't think—but if I had to guess, I'd say it must be somewhere in the foothills of The Berkshires mountain range.

It's a beautiful place where the weather is almost always perfect because nine months out of the year it's Autumn at the peak of Leaf Season. It also has a magical bubble around it which keeps anyone who doesn't have magic of their own—or isn't magical in some way—out.

Of course, I didn't know any of that. I just knew I was desperate to get away from the office and from Mr. Price and his cruel comments and arbitrary rules that reminded me so much of my abusive past. So I missed all the details like the gorgeous Fall foliage and the quaint shops lining Main Street.

My eyes were blurry with tears as I came running through the doorway which had magically appeared in place of the ladies room door back home. So blurred, in fact, that I ran right into someone as soon as I came through.

That someone was Tark and it was like running into a brick wall. I mean that literally—I bonked my head on his chest plate (he was dressed in traditional Orc armor for a festival that day)—and fell on my ass right in front of him.

"Ouch!" I cried, my hand flying to my head, which was already throbbing. Had I run into a wall? But there had never been a wall right inside the ladies room before!

"Fuck! I'm so sorry—are you all right?" an inhumanly deep voice rumbled.

An enormous figure was suddenly looming over me. An enormous *green* figure with glowing golden eyes and wild black hair that spilled around his broad shoulders. He had *fangs*, too—(I later learned these were tusks)—and he was absolutely *huge*.

I was at a serious disadvantage—disoriented and with my head still ringing from the abrupt blow I'd taken from his armor. Also, I had never been into fantasy much, so I didn't even know what the Creature looming over me was. To me, he just looked like a monster. I was so overwhelmed that when he leaned over me, trying to get a better look at the mark on my head, that I tried to scramble away.

"Hey, no, Babygirl!" Tark rumbled. Reaching for me, he scooped me into his arms.

"What are you doing? Put me down!" I gasped, struggling to get free.

But he wasn't letting me go. His arms tightened gently but firmly around me.

"I don't think so—not until I see how hurt you are."

He rose, lifting me to an immense height, and peered anxiously into my face.

At that point, it was all just too much. I felt like I had stepped from one nightmare—my boss's office—and into another one—whatever the hell *this* was. My brain overloaded like a computer that's been asked to run too many programs at once and I fainted.

The last thing I remember was seeing Tark's golden eyes staring into mine…and then everything went black.

2

HARMONY

When I woke up, I was in a dim room and for some reason I was lying almost horizontal instead of sitting up. Something hard and warm was pressed against my left side but I couldn't see it clearly—the room was too dark and my vision was blurry.

"What...where am I?" I blinked and tried to look around, which made my head ache. "Ohhhh," I moaned, clutching at it. "What's wrong with me?"

"You ran into me and bumped your head," a deep, rumbling voice informed me. "Then you blacked out."

"What...? Who...?" I peered up towards the source of the voice and saw two golden eyes looking down into mine. "Oh my God—who are you?" I demanded, my voice coming out in a gasp.

"My name is Tark—I'm a Creature—an Orc," he rumbled. "Please don't be afraid—I would never hurt you. It's just that all you humans are so small and breakable!"

"Breakable?" I didn't know what to think about that but I had other questions. "An Orc? Like…from the Lord of the Rings?"

I wasn't much into fantasy, as I said, but a friend of mine from college had gotten me to watch several of the movies with her. The guy leaning over me didn't really look like the Orcs from the popular franchise, though. He wasn't covered in oily goop for one thing and his face wasn't all misshapen and weird for another.

In fact, aside from the tusks, the glowing golden eyes, and his green skin, he looked like a normal, handsome guy. Well, if a normal guy was over eight feet tall and extremely muscular, that was. Also, he smelled really good—a kind of woodsy, spicy, masculine scent that drew me to him almost against my will. I was pretty sure the ugly baddies from the LOTR movies didn't smell like *that*.

Tark frowned at my words.

"I've heard of those movies but I haven't seen them. They don't paint my people in a very good light, I don't think."

Oh my God, had I just offended him? Were the Orcs in the Lord of the Rings like some kind of racist caricatures of his people? I immediately felt bad and guilty.

"I'm sorry, it's just that you're the first Orc I've ever met, er, in person," I said quickly. "I didn't mean to offend you."

"No offense taken," he said mildly. "I hadn't met many humans either—until I moved to Hidden Hollow."

"Hidden Hollow?" I asked and put a hand to my head again. "Ow! Is that what this place is called?"

"That is the name of the town. But for now, you are in my office."

The new voice startled me and I looked up to see a woman in a doctor's coat standing there beside me. She must have walked over when I was busy talking to Tark, because I hadn't seen her earlier.

Except when I looked at her more fully, I realized it would be impossible for her to *walk* anywhere—because the bottom half of her, from the waist down, looked like an enormous snake!

"I am Madam Healer," the snake-woman said to me. "I take it you have never been here, to Hidden Hollow before?" she added dryly, probably because my eyes were getting bigger and bigger as I looked at her.

"N-no," I stuttered. "I…I've never been here before. Or seen anyone like you—either of you," I added, looking back at Tark. The huge Orc was still cradling me like a baby in his arms and I had never felt so helpless—so vulnerable—in my life.

Madam Healer made what sounded like a hissing sigh and I saw a forked tongue flicker out from between her perfectly lipsticked lips.

"Ah, she is a virgin human," she remarked, clearly speaking to Tark. "The town is drawing in so many of them lately!"

"Er, I'm *not* a virgin," I said quickly, wondering if they were looking for some kind of virgin sacrifice for some reason. Of course, I hadn't been with many guys either—I had a grand total of two ex-lovers, though the last one hardly counted since he had gotten drunk and passed out halfway through. However, the first one had been successful —I most definitely was *not* a virgin.

But Madam Healer was shaking her head.

"No, my dear—that wasn't my meaning at all."

"Madam Healer means you're a human who doesn't know anything about magic," Tark explained. "And you're probably surprised to be here, in Hidden Hollow."

"Surprised is an understatement," I admitted. "I was trying to get to the ladies room so I could have a good cry!"

"And instead you ran into me." Tark smiled down at me, (a surprisingly friendly expression considering the tusks.)

"Um, yes. I guess I did," I said cautiously. "Look, I really need to get up." I tried to sit up and he helped me, lifting his arm to raise my head.

I promptly groaned.

"Oh, why does it hurt so much?" I moaned, touching the lump on my forehead with my fingers.

"Probably because of the pain and damage spell on my armor." Tark sounded apologetic. "Sorry—it's supposed to hurt enemies only. I guess it mistook you for one, since you came rushing at me through the magic door."

There was too much going on in that statement for me to even form a question about it, but I tried anyway.

"Are you saying your armor knows if you have an enemy after you?" I demanded weakly.

"That's just the way it's spelled," Tark explained. "Like I said, if you hadn't come running at me, it never would have hurt you."

"Enough of this—let me look at the girl. Bring her to my exam room," Madam Healer demanded.

"Yes, Madam Healer," Tark rumbled. And before I could make any moves to get out of his arms and stand on my own, he was lifting me and cradling me to his chest as he followed the snake-lady further into the dimness.

At last we went into a slightly brighter area. There was a counter and sink with some open-form cabinets on one wall. The cabinets were filled with all kinds of bottles and jars, some with mysterious, sparkly contents and others with murky dark liquid inside. There was a rectangular, unpadded exam table in the center of the room.

"Sit her here—unless you prefer to hold her?" Madam Healer said, looking up at Tark.

"I'll hold her," he said firmly, without even asking me.

I started to protest, but the exam table didn't look very comfortable and I wasn't sure I trusted the snake-lady. Oddly, I *did* seem to trust the huge Orc who was holding me, though I couldn't have said why. He just seemed...*safe*. I know that doesn't make any sense, considering how he looked, but that was how he *felt*. So I didn't make a fuss as he cradled me in his arms.

Madam Healer leaned over me and produced a light which she shined in my eyes.

"Hmm, pupils are normal," she pronounced and frowned at me. "How are you feeling now? Do you still have pain in your head?"

"Only when I touch it." I pressed my fingertips lightly to the bump on my forehead and winced. "Ouch!"

"Hmm...a lingering effect of the spelled armor, I think," she remarked. "Let me get a counterspell healing potion—that should take care of things."

She slithered over to the cabinets and looked through them thoughtfully before taking down a slim bottle that appeared to be half full of sparkly purple liquid.

"Dear me—almost out," I heard her murmur to herself. Then she poured most of the contents of the bottle into what looked like a martini glass and brought it over to me. "Here—drink this," she said, trying to hand it to me.

But I refused to take the drink.

"I don't think so!" I protested. "I'm not going to take anything until you tell me *exactly* what's in it. I'm training to be a pharmacist—I know better than to take unknown substances."

"A pharmacist, is it?" Madam Healer gave me an interested look. "I believe that is the human version of an apothecary or an alchemist, is it not?"

"I don't know—I guess maybe," I said guardedly. "But the point is, I'm *not* drinking it until I know what's in it."

Madam Healer nodded graciously.

"Very well—as you are not in grave or immediate danger and I have no other patients to treat at the moment, I will explain the ingredients and the spells that went into this particular potion."

She made a gesture and suddenly an old-fashioned chalk board about as big as a white board appeared beside her.

I gasped at the sudden appearance and felt Tark's arms tighten around me protectively. But Madam Healer only smiled and let her forked tongue slip out—which I later learned was her version of laughing.

"Please don't worry—I don't have much magic that isn't of the healing variety, so I had one of the witches in town make this spell for me. It comes in handy whenever I need to explain something in writing," she said. "Now please—attend to me."

What followed was the most complex and fascinating chemistry lesson I'd ever had. Only it wasn't actually chemistry like I'd learned in any of my classes at USF back home—it was *magical* chemistry.

Madam Healer started out simply by listing the ingredients of the potion and then she got more in-depth, writing out their chemical formulas and explaining the spell that was used to weave each one together before they were all added to a single pot and "melded" as she called it.

She seemed surprised when I kept up with her lesson and asked pertinent questions.

"My...no one has ever understood it so well before!" she said. "You must be at the very top of your class back home in the Human Realm, my dear."

"I have a 4.0 GPA," I said, unable to keep the pride out of my voice. "But this isn't like any chemistry I've ever learned before."

"Of course not—but you're doing quite amazingly well anyway." She sighed. "Much better than the last apprentice I tried to train. That boy simply could *not* get his head around the material."

I could see how someone might have a problem with the potion formula. It really was complex—which was what made it fascinating, as far as I was concerned. It also made Madam Healer's next question easier to answer.

"Now that you understand it, will you take a sip of the healing potion?" she asked. "I promise it will take away the magical ache from the spelled armor. Your headache will be gone like *that.*" And she snapped her fingers—which were covered in tiny scales, like the rest of her body—dramatically.

"All right. I'll take a sip," I agreed. "Er, but can I stand up first?"

"Better not—what if you get dizzy?" Tark rumbled. It occurred to me that the Orc was extremely strong. He had been holding me patiently all this time, though the lecture had taken almost thirty minutes, but he still seemed reluctant to put me down. And, as I think I mentioned before, I'm not exactly skinny so it couldn't have been easy to hold me like a baby all this time—though he certainly made it *look* easy.

"Tark is right—just take a sip for now." And Madam Healer held the martini glass filled with shimmering purple liquid carefully to my lips. "He can put you down when you feel better."

I took a careful sip and was surprised at the light, delicious flavor that rolled over my tongue.

"Oh—it actually tastes good! Like some kind of candied flower petals."

Madam Healer smiled and her forked tongue slipped out from between her perfect lips for a moment.

"Ah yes—I take great pride in the flavor of my potions. It's not always easy finding non-magical ingredients that won't react with the magic ones to create a pleasant taste. *Now* try touching your head, my dear," she added, gesturing to my forehead. "Does it feel better?"

Carefully, I put my fingers to the lump on my forehead…only to find it was mostly gone.

"Oh—it *does* feel better!" I exclaimed. "Wow—I've never had any medicine that worked that fast!"

"That's because it's *magical*," she reminded me. "But having said that, I don't want you leaving Hidden Hollow right away. I need you to stay close just in case there's any kind of delayed reaction either to the potion or to the armor."

"Why—do you think there will be?" I asked, feeling suddenly anxious. She shook her head.

"Almost certainly not, but I wouldn't be doing my job if I let you leave the Magical Realm right away after having your very first sip of a magical potion."

"I can watch over her—she can come home with me," Tark offered quickly. "I'm close to your office so if anything happens, I can bring her right back over."

"Very well." She nodded. "Just keep her for an hour or so, will you?

If she feels fine at the end of that time, she can go back to the Mortal Realm."

"An hour?" I exclaimed as the implications of what they were saying hit me. "But I've probably already been here at least forty-five minutes—if not longer. If I stay another hour, my boss is going to be so mad at me! I mean, he already *hates* me. I need to go back right now!"

"Hates you? How could anyone *hate* you?" Tark rumbled, looking down at me with a frown.

"Don't worry my dear—I'll give you my spare time charm," Madam Healer remarked. She went to the shelves again and this time she came back with a slim golden band that looked a little like a watch. It had a face with all the numbers of the clock marked on it and two black hands. The time it was telling seemed correct, but there was no glass over the face to keep the hands protected.

"How does it work?" I asked, as she wound it around my wrist.

"Just push back the hour hand to reset the time to when you wish it to be," she explained. "Then you'll go back to that time. But I'm afraid it can't go further back than three hours," she added. "I use it when I have a lot of patients and I'm running late. That way I can see everyone at their appointed time and no one is inconvenienced."

I couldn't help wishing that doctors in the "Human Realm" as they called it had access to that kind of equipment.

"But if I turn back time, does that mean I'll forget everything that happened here in, er, Hidden Hollow?" I asked uncertainly.

As bizarre as this experience was, I wanted to remember it, I realized. Literally running into Tark and meeting Madam Healer and the strange but fascinating magical chemistry lesson—all of it was something I never wanted to forget. It was weird but amazing—I wanted to think it over later when I finally got home and slipped into bed.

"That's an *excellent* question, my dear," Madam Healer said approvingly. "But since you apparently have magic in your blood, no, I do not believe you will forget our encounter."

"Magic in my blood?" I frowned. "No, you must be mistaken. I don't have any magic at all." If I had, I was thinking, my life would probably have been a whole lot happier and a hell of a lot easier.

"Ah, but you *must,*" Madam Healer said earnestly. "Otherwise Hidden Hollow would never have called to you and the magical bubble that surrounds the town would not have parted to allow you entrance."

"Magical bubble?" I asked, frowning. But just as Madam Healer was opening her mouth to answer, there was a tinkling sound from the front room.

"Ah—I'm afraid I have another patient," she said. "But I would greatly like to talk to you again, my dear…er, what is your name?"

"Oh—Harmony. I'm Harmony," I said.

"Harmony. I believe your magic may lie in the same vein as my own," she said. "Come talk to me later and we can discuss it." She looked up at Tark. "You will watch over her for at least an hour?"

"Of course." He nodded. "I'll bring her right back if there's a problem."

"Do that." She nodded at me again and then slithered out of the room, leaving me still cradled in the massive Orc's arms.

3

HARMONY

Tark took me to his house—which was only two houses over from Madam Healer's office, just off Main Street—and put me down at last, carefully on his enormous couch.

"How do you feel?" he asked anxiously, sitting down beside me.

"Um…okay, I guess." I touched my forehead again. The lump was completely gone by now and I doubted I was going to have any kind of reaction. I knew, at least with human medications, that if there's going to be a bad reaction, it will normally happen right away. So it was probably safe for me to go home now.

But I didn't want to.

There was something about the big Orc sitting beside me—something I liked and trusted. I didn't want to say goodbye to him just yet.

Meanwhile, Tark was making himself more comfortable.

"If you don't mind, I'm going to take this fucking thing off," he rumbled and rose to remove the elaborately carved silver plate that covered his broad chest.

When it came off, I had to bite back a gasp. It was molded, like a lot of armor is, to show defined pecs and abs, but I didn't know what might be under it. But from what I could see through the thin white T-shirt he was wearing, it looked like his chest was even *better* defined than the armor that had been covering it. He was pure muscle—and completely mouthwatering in an extra-extra-extra large way.

"Sorry—I was getting kind of sweaty," he apologized and plucked at the t

T-shirt with a grimace.

"Er, you can take it off—if you want. The shirt, I mean," I added quickly. "I won't be offended."

"Oh, if you don't mind," he rumbled and proceeded to peel the thin white shirt up and off.

I tried not to stare—I *really* did. But it was really hard not to. He looked like a Greek god—if Greek gods were green, that was. I noticed with interest that the flat disks of his nipples were a darker green than his skin and that he didn't have any chest hair. He did, however, have a narrow line of black hair that led from his navel down into the waistband of his brown leather trousers.

"I'd better get something else to wear," he said and started for the back of the house, which I hadn't seen yet. Then he stopped. "Or maybe I'd better not. What if you have a reaction while I'm gone?"

"You can just stay here—I don't mind if you're shirtless," I said, which was possibly the biggest understatement I'd ever been guilty of. I was enjoying the sight of his bare chest and broad shoulders way more than I should have—especially since he was basically a stranger.

It occurred to me belatedly that I ought to be afraid—not just because he was so much bigger and stronger than me, but because I was in the home of a strange man. Or a strange Orc, I guess. But I didn't feel the sense of threat I might have if I'd been with a human guy—I can't explain why, I just knew that Tark wouldn't hurt me. Maybe it was because he'd just spent almost forty-five minutes holding me gently against his chest and making sure I was okay—those weren't the actions of a serial killer.

"Would you like something to drink?" he asked me.

"Uh, sure—what do you have?" I said.

"Well, I *think* I have some wine. And some Pixie Punch. Or just water," he offered.

"Water is fine," I said. It seemed like the safest choice. I didn't want to be drinking wine when I was about to go back to work and I had no idea what "Pixie Punch" was.

"I'll go get it." He got up again and then hesitated, clearly not wanting to leave me. Obviously he took his duty to watch over me very seriously.

"How about if I come with you?" I offered. "You can show me your kitchen—if you don't mind."

"Sure, you can have the tour. Come on, then."

"Okay." I started to slide off the couch—it was too high for me to get off normally. But Tark surprised me by reaching down and taking me by the waist to lift me down gently.

"Sorry," he said as he set me down. "I should have asked first. I just didn't want you to get hurt."

"I'm fine. And I didn't mind," I said. And surprisingly, I didn't. In fact, I kind of liked it. I had never dated a human guy who could pick me up like that or one who could make me feel dainty and petite just by standing beside me. Tark did both of those things easily—it made me like him even more.

"Oh, good," he said, looking relieved. "Well come on, let me give you the tour."

He took me through his whole house and I got to see his enormous dining room table and chairs as well as a bathroom with a toilet high enough that I would need a step ladder to get up on it. He also opened his bedroom door and I got a glimpse of where he slept—a bed that put any California King to shame.

"Wow—that's big enough for eight people to sleep in!" I remarked.

Tark made a rumbling noise that I thought might be a laugh.

"Not if they're my size! Though I could fit someone *your* size, I'm sure," he remarked, giving me an appraising look with half-lidded eyes.

"Oh, well..." I began uncertainly.

"Sorry—did I offend you? I'm never sure with humans—your kind is really new to me," he said.

"No, no—I just...I'm *not* going to sleep with you," I said bluntly, not sure how else to put it. "We need to get that straight right now."

"No, of course not," he said, looking surprised. "I was just making a joke, that's all. We barely fucking know each other and I haven't even prepared you."

"Prepared me?" I frowned uncertainly.

"You know—I haven't kissed you, touched you..." He gave me another long look. "Tasted you."

"Uh, tasted me?" I wondered uneasily if he meant that in a "grind your bones to make my bread" kind of way, like a giant in a fairytale.

"You know, I haven't kissed and licked between your legs," he said, as though it was obvious. "What do humans call it?"

"Oh, um..." I could feel my cheeks getting hot as I suddenly pictured him licking my pussy, which was suddenly feeling extremely hot and achy. "Going down, I guess?" I suggested, shifting and pressing my thighs together tightly.

"Now your face is getting red—that means you're embarrassed, right?" he asked, frowning. "Did I say something humans consider rude?"

"Not *exactly*..." I cleared my throat. "It's just that we humans don't usually talk about, er, sexual things until we get to know someone really well."

"Sorry!" He sighed and rubbed a hand over his bristly jaw. "Orcs talk about sex whenever and to whoever—it's natural, you know? But I didn't mean to make you feel uncomfortable. I won't say anything else like that."

"It's okay," I said. "Er, maybe we should just move on from the bedroom."

"Good idea." He swung the bedroom door shut so I couldn't see the massive bed anymore and continued the tour. There wasn't much else to see though, since the house was just one level, and we ended up in the kitchen.

Tark opened a massive refrigerator and I saw what looked like several take-out containers, lots of vegetables, a bottle of wine, and a jug with a stopper in it.

"Is that the, uh, Pixie Punch?" I asked, pointing to it.

"Yeah, but it's pretty potent stuff," he said, removing another pitcher—a clear glass one that was half full of water. "Don't know why I offered it to you—it'd knock a tiny little thing like you on your ass."

"I might surprise you," I said, putting a hand on my hip. "Can I just try a sip?"

I didn't know what had gotten into me. I shouldn't be *offering* to drink alcohol at a strange Orc's house! If I was with a human man, it would be like asking to get date-raped.

Tark seemed to consider, but then he shook his head.

"I don't think so, Babygirl. It wouldn't be safe—not with you having the other magic potion in your system."

"*What* did you call me?" I frowned up at him. It occurred to me that I halfway remembered him calling me that when I had first run into him, but I had been too upset to protest.

"Oh, sorry," he apologized. "It's just a nickname for a little one and you know you're just so *tiny*."

I really did feel like a kid, standing there in his massive kitchen where all the countertops came up past my breasts and the oven looked big enough to roast and entire pig in at once. But I didn't like to admit it.

"I'm *not* little," I protested. "I'm really tall for a woman—I'm almost five foot eleven. And I'm not skinny either."

"Thank goodness you're not," he rumbled. "So many of the human women I see look like they might get blown away in a storm."

"The point is, I'm *not* little," I repeated.

He gave that rumbling laughter again.

"Maybe not to a human male. For me you're the size of a…well, a babygirl. But I won't call you that if you don't want me to."

"I'm…not exactly sure how I feel about it," I admitted. "How about that water, since you won't let me try the Pixie Punch?"

"I'll let you have some next time you come—if you visit again," he offered. "I just want to be sure you're all right with that potion you took."

I was touched by his concern for me. I wondered if all Orcs were this nice to women. If so, they were getting a bad rap in the Lord of the Rings movies.

He poured me a glass of water which was so big I had to wrap both my hands around it. Luckily he only filled it half full but it was still much more than I could drink. It was cold and refreshing, though. I told him so as I reached to put the glass in his sink.

"Here—let me—the sink is deep and your arms aren't that long, Babygirl," he murmured, taking it from me.

This time I didn't say anything about the nickname—I think I had already decided I kind of liked it.

We walked back to sit on the couch together but when I started to scramble up onto it, Tark lifted me again, without asking.

"Thank you." I settled and he sat beside me, closer this time. "So tell me about the magical world," I said to him. "This town, er—"

"Hidden Hollow," he supplied.

"Oh, right. Hidden Hollow. Are you *sure* it doesn't let non-magical people in?" I asked. "Because I'm pretty positive there's nothing special or magical about me."

"Oh, I wouldn't bet on that," he rumbled and I noticed that his golden eyes were glowing as he looked me swiftly up and down before his gaze came back to my face. "I think you're *very* special."

I could feel myself blushing again at his frank appraisal and praise. I wasn't used to men looking at me that way. Honestly, I was more or less used to being invisible.

Whenever I went out with my friends—who were all thin—I was

always the wingman. Always the one the guys ignored. It was like they didn't see me. Or if they *did* bother to talk to me, it was always asking for advice on how to get one of my skinny friends to date them. I was sick of it, but that's the existence of a curvy girl—it sucks to date when you're bigger.

But Tark was looking at me like *I* was one of my skinny friends—like I was the beautiful one, not just someone to ignore and pass over. It made me blush but I have to admit, I also liked it—I liked it a *lot*.

"Well, thank you," I said, putting a hand to my cheek—it was hot. "But I mean, I don't think there's anything *magical* about me."

"Just because you haven't discovered your magic yet doesn't mean you don't have it," he pointed out. "We have people showing up here all the time who don't know what their magic is. But they always find it—I'm sure you will too. If you come back," he added.

"I think I'd like to come back," I said, which was true. "But, er, I don't know how I got here in the first place."

"You said something about trying to get into a room full of ladies?" he said, frowning. "But I don't know—that was after you bumped your head."

"Oh—the *ladies* room!" I couldn't help laughing. "That's just a nice word for the bathroom."

"Oh—that makes more sense." He nodded thoughtfully, then frowned. "But you said you were going there to cry—was that right?"

"Um..." I nibbled my lower lip, wondering if I should tell him.

Normally, I wouldn't have told anyone, not even my friends. I hated being pitied. But somehow, Tark felt like a safe space—I found I *wanted* to tell him.

"It was my boss," I admitted at last. "He said...some pretty nasty things to me and threw some things at me and, well...sometimes you just can't help crying, you know?"

"He *what?*" The angry tone in his deep voice surprised me. "What did he throw at you? What did he say?"

"It was just some papers," I said quickly, surprised at how upset he'd gotten on my behalf. "He, uh, claimed that he told me to alphabetize them—only he didn't! He's always making up new rules and not telling me about them until I've broken them somehow."

I couldn't keep the irritation out of my voice. Sometimes working for Mr. Price was nearly unbearable!

"He sounds like a fucking *asshole*," Tark growled and suddenly his face was scary again. Or it *would* have been scary if I'd thought his anger was directed at me—it wasn't, though. I knew that instinctively and I wasn't frightened.

"He *is* an asshole," I said and sighed. "But he's an asshole I'm stuck with for the next four years—at least until I finish school."

"What? Why are you stuck with him?" Tark demanded. "You ought to leave that job!"

"I can't," I said and proceeded to explain about the contract I'd signed and the way I couldn't get out of it because I didn't have an extra hundred thousand or so to spend.

Through it all, Tark listened intently. What I really appreciated was the fact that he *didn't* start offering solutions right away—though he did ask why, even if I had to stay at Bentley Pharmaceuticals, I couldn't at least get away from Mr. Price.

When I explained that I'd tried and HR wouldn't let me leave him because Mr. Price didn't want to let me go, his face went as dark as a thundercloud.

"That asshole is a Sin Sucker!" he growled.

"I'm sorry—a what?" I asked, raising my eyebrows.

"A Sin Sucker—a being that enjoys the discomfort or pain of others," he explained. "Most Sin Suckers feed on physical pain, but there are plenty out there that feed on emotional pain too."

"But that's here in the Magical Realm," I pointed out. "I'm sure we don't have anything like that in the human world—do we?"

"You sure as fuck do," he said, frowning. "In fact, you had a whole lot of them back in the 1940s. What do you think the fucking Nazis were?"

"Really?" I looked at him, wide-eyed. "You're saying there were magical creatures living in among us, uh, humans?"

"Don't lump yourself in with the humans when you've obviously got magical talent," he told me. "And yes, there were and there still are. Most of them wear glamours to disguise themselves so humans don't notice them. Like, most of your movie stars are fairies, hiding their wings and their pointed ears with magic. And the billionaires and CEOs are almost all dragons—hoarding more wealth than they could ever possibly use just so no one else can have it. So why shouldn't your asshole boss be a magical creature too?"

"I really doubt he is," I said, thinking of Mr. Price's skinny frame and the way he always wore his reading glasses perched on the very end of his long, bony nose. If there was anyone less magical than him, I didn't know who it would be. Except maybe me—I was sure the fact that I'd gotten into Hidden Hollow in the first place must be some kind of cosmic mistake.

But talking about my boss made me glance at the time charm that Madam Healer had given me…and realize that I had been in the magical little town for almost three hours.

"Oh, I really need to be going!" I said. "But…I don't know how to get home."

"Or how to get back again—if you want to," Tark pointed out. He reached for my hand. "I mean, *if* you want to."

"I do want to," I said honestly, squeezing his long fingers. His hand was so much bigger than mine I felt like a kid again, holding hands with an adult. But it was nice—*really* nice. There was a spark between us—I could feel it. And that wasn't something I could say about any of the human men I'd dated—not that there had been very many.

"I want you to, too, Babygirl," he rumbled. "Come on—I know who we can talk to about it."

He rose and lifted me off the couch, just like he had before. Then he frowned down at himself.

"Just let me throw on a shirt, okay?"

"Sure." I nodded, though I was sad not to see his bare chest anymore. He really *was* mouthwatering.

But I wasn't too disappointed when he came back. He was wearing a black T-shirt that clung lovingly to his chest and abs and a pair of jeans that showed an impressively muscular ass. Damn, did all Orcs look this good or was he addicted to the gym? I didn't know, but either way, he was hot!

I didn't have much time to admire him, though because he was already taking my hand in his.

"Come on, Babygirl—let's see about getting you home…and bringing you back again," he told me.

And then he led me out the door and into Hidden Hollow.

4

HARMONY

This time I got to notice things I hadn't when he was carrying me back and forth before. The crisp Fall weather gave me a chill since I was just wearing a thin silk button down blouse, but I liked it. I shivered in delight as a cool gust of wind rushed through the colorful treetops and swirled around my body.

"Oh—it's actually cold!"

"Of course it is—it's Fall. It's almost always Fall here—fucking nice," Tark rumbled. "It's my favorite season. But are you cold, Babygirl? Here…"

He put one long arm around me and drew me closer to his side. I slipped my own arm around his waist, glad to get closer to him. He smelled so good and he really was warm—his big body put out heat like a furnace.

But the walk didn't last long. We passed by several shops, including a kind of supermarket called "Kreature's Emporium and Fine Groceries" and then Tark led me up the front steps of what looked like a sprawling Bed and Breakfast.

There was a sign out front that read, "The Red Lion Inn" and by the door was an outline of a lion's head in red paint.

"Goody Albright runs this place," Tark explained. "She helped me get settled when I first came to town—she can help you too, I'm sure."

When he opened the front door, we stepped into what looked like a piece of history. There were portraits on the walls that looked hundreds of years old and lots of antique furniture. The rugs on the dark hardwood floor were well-worn but also obviously antique.

A woman—at least I *thought* she was a woman—came bustling up to us. She had brown, bark-like skin and the arms and legs that stuck out from her dress were almost stick-like with big, knobby elbows and knees. Her nose was long and crooked and there was a single green leaf growing from one side of it.

"Yes, how can I help you?" she asked in a businesslike way.

"We're here to see Goodie Albright," Tark said. "Tell her it's Tark, calling in his favor."

"She owes you a favor?" I asked, looking up at him as the peculiar attendant hurried away.

He nodded.

"I fixed some things for her around the inn. And she had a really big boulder she wanted moved to make way for a new cabin but it was magically rooted so she couldn't use a spell. So I moved it for her."

"Really? How big was it?" I asked.

Tark shrugged and held a hand up to about his eye-line.

"Oh, about this tall, I guess. And twice as big around. It wasn't easy to shift but once I got started, it rolled pretty well."

"Wow—you must be *really* strong," I remarked. "I mean, I knew you were—you were holding me at the, uh, doctor's office for over half an hour without even breaking a sweat. But still…"

"What? You're light as a feather, Babygirl." He grinned down at me, showing off his pearly white tusks. "I could hold you all day."

"Oh, um…" I was starting to blush again when a new person entered the room.

Goody Albright had curly gray hair and she was wearing a colorful dress that might have been a dressing gown or a robe—it was hard to say. It was covered in a mint green and peacock blue paisley pattern and her cat-eyed glasses were turquoise to match.

"Well hello, Tark—what's this I hear about you calling in your favor?" she asked, smiling at both of us. She might have been anywhere between forty-six to seventy-six—she had a kind of agelessness about her, despite the fine wrinkles at the corners of her eyes and mouth.

"Just what it sounds like. Goody Albright, this is Harmony…er—I don't know your last name, I just realized that," he said to me.

"Oh, Ward. I'm Harmony Ward," I said, holding out a hand to her.

"Delighted to meet you, my dear. By the way you're looking around, I can tell this is your first visit to Hidden Hollow," she said, smiling graciously as she shook with me.

"Yes, it is," I admitted. "But I'm not quite sure how I got here. Or how to get home. Or how to get back here again when I want to," I added, casting a glance at Tark.

"Ahh, I see. Yes indeed—come with me and we'll figure it out together." She held out a hand to me but I hesitated.

"Er, I don't mean to be rude, but I don't have much time," I told her. "Madam Healer gave me a time charm, but it's only good for going back three hours and I've nearly spent that much time here already."

"I see." She nodded. "Let me see the charm please."

I held up my arm and she tapped the golden charm wrapped around my wrist three times and nodded.

"There. That added another hour. Now please come with me—we'll go sit on my back porch and have some tea while we talk."

Tark and I followed her through the winding maze of the inn—which turned out to be the oldest still-standing inn in the whole country as Goodie Albright proudly informed us.

"It's been here since the witch trials in Salem," she told me. "That was when magical folks started congregating here in Hidden Hollow—to get away from the madness of the Human Realm. And lately more and more magic users are being drawn here—because once again, the outside world is getting very strange and scary."

I thought of the things I'd been seeing on the news lately and couldn't help agreeing with her. The "Human Realm" as she called it, was getting awfully frightening of late. It was nice to think there was a cozy magical sanctuary tucked away and safe from all the craziness.

"That's nice, but I really don't think I have any magic," I told Goodie Albright. "I mean, everyone keeps telling me I do, but I've never done anything magical or special in my life."

"Perhaps your magic is still sleeping in your blood. Or it was, until you needed it—and needed to get away to Hidden Hollow," she told me. "We'll soon find out."

We got settled at a small table on a glassed-in porch in the back of the inn. Well, Goodie Albright and I did, at any rate. She had to call for a reinforced stool for Tark to sit on—it took two brownies (that was the name of the attendants with the bark-like skin) to lug it over to the table we were sitting at.

I couldn't help admiring the view—just outside the porch was a gorgeous garden that was somehow in full bloom despite the Fall weather. Flowers and vegetables and fruits all mingled together in a glorious tangle that didn't appear to have any rhyme or reason but still looked amazingly well tended.

Once we were all seated, Goodie Albright called for tea and something else.

"My magic-testing kit—it's in the second drawer in my office," she told the brownie, who ran quickly to go get it.

The tea tray arrived with a steaming china pot and three cups as well as a plate full of delicious looking cookies. At the same time, another brownie brought what looked like a row of three test tubes standing upright in a wooden tray. One was filled with silvery dust, the second had golden glitter, and the third was empty.

"Now then, Tark would you mind pouring while I test Harmony's magic?" she said.

"Happy to," the big Orc rumbled. He looked down at me. "Milk and sugar, right?"

"How did you know how I like my tea?" I asked.

He grinned at me.

"You just seem like the milk and sugar type, but wanted to be sure."

I wasn't sure what that meant but before I could ask anything else, Goodie Albright was asking for my hand.

"What are you going to do?" I asked nervously, because she had produced a long, extremely sharp-looking needle from somewhere.

"I'm going to test your blood to see how much magic you have," she said simply. "I'm sure you have some—enough to get you here, anyway." She frowned. "By the way—did a key appear for you before you came to Hidden Hollow?"

"A key? No." I shook my head. "I thought I was going into the ladies room—the bathroom, I mean," I corrected myself. "But instead, I wound up here."

She raised her eyebrows in surprise.

"Hmm—so you didn't even need a key to enter? This should be interesting."

She pricked my index finger quickly and then held it over the empty test tube. She squeezed the tiny wound until three drops of blood had fallen into the tube and then wrapped my finger in a small strip of soft linen.

"There—that will stop the bleeding in a minute. Now, let's see…"

She started by sprinkling a bit of the shiny silver dust from the first test tube over the blood at the bottom of the third test tube.

At once something started happening—the blood turned green, then yellow and began to glow.

"Ah—interesting!" Goodie Albright nodded to herself. "And now let's see how it reacts with *this*."

She sprinkled some of the golden glitter from the second test tube over the glowing blood and then gave a little gasp.

I gasped too and so did Tark because the reaction was swift and immediate. The golden yellow liquid turned into a kind of semi-solid foam and began to expand so fast it shot out of the top of the tube.

More and more of it came shooting out—like someone squeezing a tube of toothpaste as fast as they could.

It was like some kind of chemical reaction, I couldn't help thinking. Only I guessed it was a magical reaction in this case.

"Goodness!" Goodie Albright exclaimed and then she said a word I couldn't understand—though I felt like I should be able to for some reason—and made a hand gesture. At once, all the glowing stuff that had grown from my blood disappeared and the test tube where it had been was suddenly empty.

"What the fuck was all *that?*" Tark growled, raising his eyebrows.

"That was proof that your new friend has *plenty* of magic in her blood," Goodie Albright said briskly. "I hope you didn't spill the tea—did you?"

Tark hadn't. He handed us our cups and I took a sip and sighed with pleasure. It had a sweet cinnamon flavor and the warm liquid running down my throat was soothing and delicious.

"So I really *do* have magic?" I said, after taking another sip. "If that's true, how come it's never come out before?"

"Magic works in mysterious ways," Goodie Albright said, smiling. "Some witches don't discover they have magic until they're well into their later years. You're lucky my dear—you found yours earlier than that."

"But what good does it do me if I don't know how to use it?" I asked. "I don't even know how to get back home again."

"Oh, that's easy enough. Here." She unpinned a broach from the lapel of her robe and handed it to me. I took it and examined it. It was shaped like a tiny silver key, about an inch long, with diamond chips imbedded in the head of it.

"I can't take this!" I protested. "It looks really valuable."

"Then just consider it a loan," Goodie Albright told me. "As long as you're wearing it, all you have to do in order to get back and forth between Hidden Hollow and the Human Realm is just draw a door in the air with your finger. The door will become solid and lead you back to the place you want to be."

"Really?" I looked down at the tiny key cupped in my hand in surprise.

"Really," she asserted. "And I hope you'll be a frequent visitor, my dear. If you keep coming back, you should eventually find out what kind of magic you have."

"Madam Healer said she thought maybe Harmony's magic was like hers," Tark offered. He had already drunk two cups of tea and was pouring himself a third. The china teacup looked like a toy from a child's tea set in his big hand.

"She did, did she? And what caused her to think that, I wonder?" Goodie Albright gave me an appraising look.

"I'm not sure," I said but Tark had an answer.

"Harmony wouldn't drink the healing potion until she knew what was in it," he said. "So Madam Healer explained and Harmony *understood* her."

He gave me an appreciative glance that made me blush.

"Well, I mean I *am* studying to be a pharmacist," I mumbled, feeling shy. "It wasn't *that* hard to understand."

"On the contrary, my dear, magical chemistry or alchemy as some call it, is an *extremely* difficult discipline to master," Goodie Albright said.

"I thought alchemy was turning a base metal like lead into gold," I said, frowning.

She waved a hand.

"Yes, that's what it *used* to mean, back in the Dark Ages. But now it's come to mean the same thing as chemistry does in the Human Realm. And as I said, it's not easy to learn. So you may have an aptitude there."

"How would I find out if I do?" I asked, intrigued.

"Well the person in town who knows the most about it is obviously

Madam Healer," she said, taking another sip of her tea. "She doesn't just heal people—she also brews most of her own potions. I'd recommend you come back to town and make an appointment to talk to her."

I liked the idea of speaking more with the snake-lady doctor. She'd been frightening at first, but after getting to know her a little, I could tell she was a very good doctor and an excellent teacher as well.

"Do you think she'd be willing to talk to me? Maybe even teach me a little?" I asked.

"Of course she would!" Goodie Albright exclaimed. "And just so you know, I've heard she's still looking for an apprentice."

"Oh, but I'm not looking for a job," I protested. "I'm kind of stuck in the job I have now. In the, uh, Human Realm."

"Ah, that's a great pity." Goody Albright sighed and shook her head. "You have so much magic in your blood, my dear—you shouldn't waste it on the humans."

"Hey, some of my best friends are humans," I protested. "In fact, *all* of them are. And I am too, for that matter."

"No, you're not—you're a witch," she said with absolute certainty.

"I'm really not," I said. "I don't own a black cat or know how to do any spells or—"

"No, no, my dear—that's just a crude stereotype. A witch is simply any human female with magic in her blood. Just as a warlock is any human male with magic," she said and offered me the plate of cookies. "Here—have one."

"Oh no, I shouldn't," I said regretfully—they really did look delicious. "I'm on a diet."

"A die-*what?*" Tark, who had been listening silently, frowned down at me.

"A *di-et.* I mean I'm trying to lose some weight," I told him.

"But why?" He looked confused. "I don't understand—why are you trying to lose your curves?"

"She's trying because human men don't like them," Goodie Albright answered for me, saving me some embarrassment, for which I was grateful.

"They don't? Well, what the fuck is wrong with them?" Tark demanded, scowling.

"Don't ask me—I'll never understand non-magical humans." Goodie Albright shrugged and offered me the cookie plate once more. "Forget about those human males my dear—they're not worth bothering about."

"Go on, Babygirl," Tark urged me, when I started to demure again. "You have as many as you want—your curves are fucking beautiful. Don't lose them because those idiotic human males are too stupid to see that!"

Blushing, I took a cookie and bit into it. It really was good—buttery and rich. It melted on my tongue but I barely tasted it. I was too busy stealing glances at the huge Orc at my side.

Nobody had ever told me my curves were beautiful before. The only compliment I ever got was the one that goes something like this: "You have such a pretty face/skin/hair! If you'd just lose a little weight, you'd be a knockout!"

I'd been hearing that same thing or variations on it since junior high. Nobody had ever told me I looked good just the way I was. I wondered if Tark really meant it—but he seemed sincere. Especially when he coaxed me to take a second cookie.

We talked a little more but much sooner than I liked, my extra hour was up and it was time to leave.

"Can I go right from here?" I asked Goodie Albright, touching the tiny silver key that I had pinned to my blouse.

"Hmm, you *could* but it would probably be better if you come and go from Main Street," she told me. "That way if you want to come in the middle of the night, you won't wake anyone at the Red Lion up."

"Oh, because I'll come back to the place I left from?" I guessed.

"Exactly." She smiled at me. "Do you know your way to the front door? I can have one of the brownies take you if you like."

"I'll take her," Tark said, rising. He offered me a hand and pulled me lightly from my chair. I got the idea he would have liked to swing me into his arms again, but he resisted the urge. "Come on, Babygirl," he rumbled. "Let's go."

We wound our way through the Red Lion Inn again until we came out the front door onto the broad front porch. There I stopped to admire the view. I had been in Hidden Hollow for so long that the sun was sliding down behind the trees, setting the gold and crimson and vermillion leaves on fire with its dying light.

It was beautiful but there was more to see than just the sunset.

Up and down the sidewalks on either side of Main Street, I saw some of the more peculiar inhabitants of the town. An ethereally lovely fairy floated by, her wings barely waving as she went. On the other side of the street, a Centaur was clopping and beside him was a Minotaur. At least I *thought* it was a Minotaur—he had a man's body and a bull's head with a silver ring through his nose.

"Oh—this town really *is* magic," I breathed, taking it all in.

"It is," Tark agreed, grinning again. "It's pretty special, isn't it? That's why I chose to move here when my Tribe kicked me out."

"They kicked you out?" I looked up at him in surprise. "Why? I mean, if you don't mind me asking."

"I don't mind." He shrugged, his broad shoulders rolling. "It's because I don't kill animals or eat their meat. They say I'm too soft hearted."

"Well, I think you're *wonderful*," I said and then blushed—should I not have said that?

But looking up at Tark's face, I was reassured. His own cheeks had gone a darker green which let me know that he was blushing too.

"Thanks, Babygirl," he rumbled and reached for my hand again. Raising it, he leaned down and placed a gentle kiss on the backs of my fingers. "I think you're pretty fucking wonderful too."

"Thank you," I whispered. My heart was suddenly pounding and I wished I dared to kiss him. If he wasn't so far away, I would have done it. Then I realized we were standing on the steps. "Hey…go down a few steps—would you?" I asked, nodding at them.

"Why?" he asked, even as he did it.

"Because…because I want to kiss you," I told him in a rush. "If…I mean, if you *want* me to."

His golden eyes blazed.

"Fuck, Babygirl—of course I want you to!"

He went down three full steps before I could reach him and even then I had to lean forward, but I did it.

Tark leaned towards me too and when our lips met, I felt it all the way down to my toes. I mean that—it was like a tingle of pure pleasure ran through my entire body and suddenly my nipples were tight and my pussy was hot and wet. In fact, I felt right on the edge of orgasm!

"Wow!" I breathed, when the kiss broke at last. "That was… *intense*."

"For me too, Babygirl." His golden eyes were half-lidded as he looked at me. "Never felt anything like that before."

"Me either," I confessed. I hadn't even noticed his tusks—maybe because he'd been being careful not to cut me with them.

We stood there for a minute longer, looking at each other, and all I wanted to do was lean forward and kiss him some more. But I was afraid if we started up again, I would never stop and I was going to be late if I didn't get back to work soon.

"Well…I guess I'd better, uh, draw a door," I said at last.

"Guess you should," Tark acknowledged, though he didn't sound happy about it.

I stepped down off the porch and went to the middle of Main Street. I felt self-conscious about doing magic right in the middle of the road, but nobody seemed to be paying attention. All the humans and Creatures just kept passing by on the sidewalks and since I didn't see a single car, I supposed the middle of the road was as safe as anywhere to draw my magic door.

Leaning down, I used my index finger like a pencil and began to drag it upward from the road.

I gasped in surprise when a glowing red line appeared as I was drawing and Tark let out a bellow of laughter.

"Hey, what's so funny?" I demanded, freezing with my finger in mid-air.

"You—you look so surprised!" He grinned at me good-naturedly. "Sorry, I shouldn't laugh. I know it's probably the first time you've ever done magic."

"It is," I said, smiling a little. It was hard to stay mad at him, even when he was laughing at me. Maybe because I could tell there was no cruelty in his laughter—no malicious intent. He was just tickled at the expression on my face.

"Well, keep going." He made a motion with his hand. "Even I know that once you start a spell you need to finish it, and I don't have any magic at all."

"What? But you're an Orc," I protested. "How can you *not* have magic?"

"Because I *am* magic," he explained. "Humans are the ones who are magic wielders. The rest of us magical folk are just Creatures—we don't have magic because we *are* magic."

This seemed confusing to me, but I didn't have time to get into a long discussion about it. I finished drawing the door and saw that it had grown a doorknob I could turn. I reached for it but before I could grab it, Tark turned me towards him. He cupped my cheek in one big hand and stroked it gently with his thumb. "There's something special about you, Babygirl—and it's not just your magic," he rumbled. "Will you promise to come back and see me again?"

"Sure." I felt my cheeks heating and my heart pounding as I looked up into his golden eyes. "Uh, when were you thinking?"

"How about tomorrow?" he suggested. "Same time as today? Or even a little later—we could have dinner together. I'll cook you a vegetarian feast."

"That sounds wonderful," I said, smiling. "I'll be here."

"I'll be waiting," he told me, dropping his hand at last. "Can't wait to see you again."

I couldn't wait to see him again, either.

5

HARMONY

I got back to the office in time to fix the documents for Mr. Price. Of course, he wasn't happy with my work—he never was—but this time I was able to let his criticism roll off my back.

"Yes, Sir. I'm sorry, Sir," I said, nodding automatically when he yelled at me.

He frowned and narrowed his watery, pale blue eyes at me.

"You seem awfully composed, Miss Ward, for someone receiving a dressing down from her superior!"

I opened my eyes wide, trying to look innocent.

"Do I? I'm sorry, Sir."

"You look just like a cow when you say that!" he snapped. "A stupid, fat cow who will never understand anything about the work we're trying to do here at Bentley Pharmaceuticals!"

I have to admit, that little piece of nastiness pierced the happy bubble I'd been walking around in ever since leaving Hidden Hollow. I could feel myself deflating.

It's so unfair—it doesn't matter how smart or accomplished you are —if you're plus-sized, some mean, nasty person can always just call you "fat" or some derivative of it and make you feel like dog shit. Even if you just won a Nobel Prize or aced your Organic Chem final or whatever. It doesn't matter the circumstances—"fat" always stings.

A mean little grin appeared on my boss's face when he saw me wilting. For the first time I wondered if Tark could be right—could he be a "Sin Sucker" after all?

But no—it was a ridiculous idea, I told myself as I left his office. I wished I could fight back—that I could tell him off once and for all. I knew what would happen if I did, though. I'd get fired and suddenly owe Bentley Pharmaceuticals over a hundred thousand dollars. Plus, I wouldn't be able to finish my degree—that would be a disaster.

So I just had to take it…which was what I did.

6

HARMONY

The next day, Mr. Price was even worse but I was buoyed by the knowledge that I would be seeing Tark that night for supper. So I was able to shake off my nasty boss's cruel words—well, *mostly*—until I could finally escape at five.

It was Friday and a lot of people had gone home early. I knew I ought to wait until I got home myself to draw the doorway to Hidden Hollow, but I just *couldn't*. It had been a hard day and I was *so* ready to see the big Orc again.

Beside the parking lot was a little piece of overgrown wilderness, which isn't uncommon in Central Florida. We live in a sub-tropical climate—the minute you stop mowing, the jungle starts growing. I stepped into the tangle of weeds and vines until I felt I was safely out of sight. Then I drew the magic door and watched eagerly as the burning red lines appeared in the air.

I can't explain the joy I felt when those lines formed! Part of me—a large part—had been afraid that my whole adventure in Hidden Hollow the day before had been some kind of illusion or maybe just a really vivid daydream. So when I saw that I was *really* going to be able to get back to the magical little town again, I felt like my heart would burst from excitement.

The door opened and I left the burning heat of the Florida Summer for the cool, crisp winds of Autumn. And standing on the other side of the door, waiting for me, was Tark.

"Babygirl!" His face broke into a broad, excited grin and he swooped down and swung me up into his arms.

He spun me around in the middle of Main Street, both of us laughing until I was dizzy. When he set me back on my feet, I nearly fell over—being swung around by a full-blooded Orc is at least as intense as being on one of those circular carnival rides.

"Hey, be careful!" Tark picked me up again, cradling me to his chest, like he had the very first time we met. "Sorry—did I make you dizzy? Are you okay?"

"I am now," I said and nuzzled against him, breathing in his warm, woodsy scent.

I couldn't help myself—I'd never felt such a deep and intense attraction to anyone in my life—not even the boy I'd given my virginity too. And I had *honestly* thought he loved me—until I found out too late that he'd only had sex with me on a bet with his friends. (Yes, I know that sounds like the plot of an awful teen drama but it really happened to me. As I found out when I heard them laughing behind the gymnasium about how "easy" it was to "fuck the fat chick".)

But enough about my sad past—I was finally happy in a way I had never expected to be. Tark carried me to his house, pausing several times to make introductions to other people and Creatures who were passing on the sidewalk. None of them seemed to think it was strange that he was carrying me and all of them were welcoming. A flighty Pixie about the size of a sparrow flew right up to me, her diaphanous wings humming so fast I couldn't see them.

"Welcome to Hidden Hollow!" she chirped in a clear, tiny voice. "You're going to love it here!"

Then she buzzed off again, making me think of Tinkerbell in the old Peter Pan movie.

The minute Tark opened his front door, a delicious aroma reached my nose.

"Mmm, that smells amazing!" I said, smiling up at him.

He smiled back.

"I hope you like braised cabbage steaks with mushroom gravy—they're kind of my specialty."

"I've never had those but if they smell like that, I can't wait," I said honestly.

"Good, but it's going to be a minute before they're ready," he said. "I didn't want to start it too early in case you came a little late. If you're not careful, the cabbage gets mushy."

"We could just talk," I offered, nodding at the couch. Or he could kiss me again—I wished he would! I was so attracted to him I felt like I couldn't keep my hands off him. I just wanted to rub up against him, like a cat in heat!

"Mmm, I guess we could," he rumbled.

He sat down on the couch, but this time he didn't put me beside him. Instead, I found myself sitting on his lap—which I confess, I really liked.

I wished I was brave enough to straddle him, but I didn't want him to think I was "easy" like the boys from so long ago had said I was. *That* had made me feel almost as bad as knowing that the guy who'd taken my virginity had made a bet that he could sleep with the "fat girl." So I just sat kind of side-saddle, facing the big Orc.

"I missed you," I told him. "I mean, I *really* missed you a lot."

"I missed you too, Babygirl," he rumbled, looking into my eyes. "I hope you don't mind sitting in my lap. You can move if you want."

"Uh-uh." I shook my head. "I like this. I mean, I like being eye-to-eye with you. You're so tall it's hard to get up to your level."

He rumbled a laugh.

"I could say that you're so short it's hard to get *down* to yours. But I like it too." Cupping my cheek, he looked into my eyes. "I really want to kiss you again."

That was exactly what I wanted, too. Threading my fingers through his coarse, black hair I pulled him down and kissed him thoroughly.

To my delight, Tark let me take the lead. He groaned softly as I explored his mouth—first with soft, closed mouth kisses—and then opened for me when I probed gently at the seam of his lips with my tongue.

I have to say that kissing a full-blooded Orc is probably what kissing a Saber Tooth Tiger would be like. Tark's teeth were sharp and lethal—I knew at once he could rip out my throat if he wanted to. But he was extra careful to be gentle with me, even when our kissing got deeper and hotter. His mouth tasted sweet and salty, a little like he'd been eating salted caramel before he came to meet me, and I couldn't get enough of it.

I *really* wanted him to touch my breasts, but again I was afraid of him thinking I was "easy." I gave him as many hints as I could, though—rubbing my breasts against his broad chest and running my fingers through his hair over and over again. I could tell he liked what I was doing by the low groans I drew from him. Finally, he pulled away.

"Goddess, baby—you're driving me fucking *crazy*." His voice was a hoarse growl and his golden eyes were lazy with lust.

"You're driving me crazy *too*," I admitted. "But I'm not done with you yet."

Feeling daring, I leaned forward and licked his neck—right under the lobe of his pointed ear. His skin was salty and delicious and his warm scent was even stronger here.

Tark sucked in a breath and groaned more loudly this time.

"*Goddess...*"

I took that as a sign that I was on the right track. My neck had always been a really sensitive area—apparently that held true for Orcs as well. At least, for Tark.

I licked and nibbled up and down the strong cords of his neck, not neglecting his long, pointed ear. When I ran the tip of my tongue along its graceful curve to the up-tilted tip, I could feel Tark's big body shivering under me. But just as I was about to nibble the lobe, he took me by the waist and pushed me gently but firmly away from him.

"What happened? Don't you like it?" I asked, feeling hurt.

Tark was breathing deeply with his eyes closed. He still had his big hands locked around my waist, so I wasn't going anywhere.

"Yeah, Babygirl—I fucking liked it. I liked it *too* much," he growled, opening his eyes at last. "Look, I don't want to take things too fast with you," he rumbled softly. "We need to be careful—*I* need to be careful."

"Careful, why?" I demanded, feeling hurt and also *extremely* sexually unfulfilled. "I won't break, you know!"

"Yes you will, if I don't watch out," he growled. Then he sighed and let go of my waist to cup my cheek in his hand. "Look, I don't want to be fucking crude, but I didn't jerk off before you came here."

"Uh…what?" I gave him a blank look.

"I should have jerked off—so I could take the edge off—before you came. That would have helped me to have more self-control," he explained. "As it is, I'm right on the edge and I don't fucking trust myself! You're too damn tempting with your gorgeous ripe tits and your soft curves rubbing against me…" He shook his head. "Don't be offended, okay? I just don't want to hurt you."

"Well…" I thought of the boulder he'd told me he'd moved and how strong he was and nodded. "Okay, I appreciate you trying to be careful with me."

"I would *never* want to hurt you," Tark rumbled. His eyes went dark. "That's another reason I left my Tribe."

"What—because they like to hurt women?" I asked, frowning.

"You could say that." He sighed and ran a hand through his shaggy black hair. "The males of my Tribe don't court a woman before they take her for a wife or a bed partner—they just fucking kidnap her. And then when they take her…well, let's just say they *aren't* gentle. I can't tell you the number of nights I lay awake when I was younger, listening to the people in the huts around mine and hearing women crying out, begging to be set free, to be…" He broke off, shaking his head. "I never wanted that. It's fucking barbaric and *wrong*. So I left. But not until I set all the women who wanted to go free. *That's* why they kicked me out—I let all of their victims go."

"I'm so sorry," I murmured, feeling chastened. "That must have been really hard for you to deal with."

"It was," he said shortly. "I just…don't want to hurt you that way—I don't want to be like the other males in my Tribe." He cupped my cheek and stroked it with his thumb. "I want to be *sweet* to you, Babygirl. I want to make you feel good but we have to take things slow."

"I understand," I said, nodding. "But really—I'm not afraid."

"You're not? Well, you *ought* to be—I'm twice your size," he said grimly. "Besides, you don't strike me as someone who's had much experience."

"I've had lovers before—two of them," I said, lifting my chin defiantly.

"Oh, *two* of them, huh? Well aren't you a woman of the world?" he said dryly. "Look, I don't care how many lovers you've had, I'm assuming they were both human—right?"

"Well, yes. A far as I know," I admitted.

"Uh-huh." He nodded. "Well let me tell you, Babygirl—being with a human is a lot different than being with an Orc. We have…different equipment."

"Really?" My eyes went wide. "Like what kind of equipment? Can I see it?"

Tark frowned.

"Eager, aren't you?"

"Oh, well…" I began blushing at once. What must he think of me? "I didn't mean—"

"Hey—it's okay." He stroked my cheek again. "Don't be

embarrassed, baby. It's okay to be curious. Just…not now. Not yet, all right? I want to get to know you first. This…what I'm feeling between us—and I think you feel it too—is special. Too special to rush."

I felt my heart swelling at his words and the soft way he was looking at me.

"Yes," I whispered. "I…I guess you're right."

"I know I'm right," he rumbled. "So for now, let's keep things above the belt. Okay?"

I nodded reluctantly.

"Okay."

"And now I'd better check the cabbage steaks," he told him. "If I don't they're going to get mushy."

7

HARMONY

Hidden Hollow had come into my life at just the right time. As my work grew more difficult and degrading, I began looking forward to my visits there more and more. I started taking lessons with Madam Healer, who seemed eager to teach me anything I wanted to learn. But even better, Tark and I saw each other regularly—almost every night—and things progressed until I felt I could confidently call him my boyfriend.

The only thing was, we hadn't slept together yet. Not that I'm super eager to hop into bed with a new guy—on the contrary, I'm usually really careful about that kind of thing. After the debacle in high school, it took me years to trust again and let myself have sex with another guy. But he was the one who got drunk and couldn't finish, as I think I mentioned before. And we broke up right after, so that was the end of that.

I had admitted my sexual history—or lack thereof—to Tark in a round-about way and he seemed to think it was my way of asking him to go slow. But after our first few dates, I didn't want to slow things down anymore—I wanted to speed them up! Every time I was with the big Orc, my body was primed and ready to go. Just smelling his warm, woodsy scent seemed to flip a switch in me that made my nipples hard and my pussy wet with sexual need.

But though we had done a lot of kissing and what my aunt would have called "heavy petting" on his enormous sofa, Tark still wouldn't do anything below the belt. And because of my inexperience, I was too shy to push him or to ask for more.

It still seemed hard to believe that someone who looked like him could want someone who looked like me. I think I was afraid that everything was going to end—that he would suddenly decide he wasn't interested anymore, which was why I was holding back from him.

These thoughts and feelings that I'd been harboring came to a head on the day when I came to his house after an especially bad time at the office. My awful boss was the cause of it, of course.

I'd been sitting in the break room eating lunch with two other executive assistants—Katrina and Jeremy. Both of them were nice enough but they weren't really friends, just acquaintances. Still, it was pleasant to have someone to eat with and talk about school, since they were under the same kind of contract I was with Bentley Pharmaceuticals. All of us were just trying to get through school without drowning in debt.

I was listening to Katrina tell us about a new show she was watching about aliens who came to Earth searching for brides when Mr. Price walked into the break room.

I froze immediately with my sandwich halfway to my mouth. It wasn't huge or disgusting—just a plain turkey on wheat and I had carrot sticks on the side. But I'd made the mistake of bringing a cupcake for dessert and it was sitting right on my plate, in front of me.

My boss walked over and got something from the break room refrigerator and I breathed a tiny sigh of relief. Maybe he was just here to get creamer for his coffee and he would leave the three of us alone.

But of course, Mr. Price couldn't do that.

He came over to our table and looked pointedly at the food on my plate, his pale eyes narrowing when he saw the cupcake.

"Well, Miss Ward, it looks like you're not even *trying* to lose weight," he remarked, frowning disapprovingly. "You know, we're developing a new weight loss drug here at Bentley—maybe I should put you in for the clinical trials. You're getting bigger by the day."

The old, familiar shame washed over me and I wanted to sink through the floor and *die*. Katrina and Jeremy just sat there. Both of them were an "acceptable" weight, so Mr. Price hadn't picked on them. I felt them staring at me with pity and probably with disgust, I thought miserably.

Why had I brought the cupcake to lunch? Why couldn't I just have a nice, normal lunch break with acquaintances without being made to feel like some kind of freak?

The minute my boss left the break room, I started gathering my things. I wasn't even halfway done with lunch but my appetite was completely gone.

"Hey, Harmony..." Katrina said tentatively. "He really shouldn't have said that. He—"

"I have to go," I mumbled, not looking at her. It seemed like if I didn't get out of there right now I was going to burst!

I threw the cupcake and the rest of my lunch in the trash and headed right for the ladies room. Forget waiting until quitting time, I needed to get away to Hidden Hollow right *now*. And thanks to the time charm, I could have at least four hours there before I had to come back and finish this miserable day.

I stepped into one of the empty stalls—the one on the end—and quickly drew the magic door. I felt a burst of relief when it opened, revealing Main Street with its cozy, quirky shops and friendly Creatures and people.

But once I stepped through, I wasn't sure what to do with myself. I didn't have a lesson planned with Madam Healer today and besides, I wasn't in the right frame of mind to learn anything new, so going to see her was out. Well, what else?

I looked around, up and down the street. Lately I'd been stopping by the local bakery—a place called The Lost Lamb, and getting myself a cupcake or a donut when I came to visit. The woman who owned it was named Celia and she was really nice. Her assistant, Sarah, was sweet too and she was married or "mated" as they called it here, to a half-Orc named Rath. I also liked the owner of the local diner, whose name was Goldie. She was quick with a joke and her coffee was the best I'd ever tasted.

But I had no interest in visiting either the diner or the bakery today. The thought of food only reminded me of how fat I was, even though I had actually *lost* some weight since I'd started dating Tark. (I guess eating vegetarian really is good for you.)

Not having anywhere else to go, I made my way to the big Orc's house. I wasn't really in the right frame of mind to see him, either. But I couldn't bear the thought of going back to the office so soon and I didn't really have anywhere else to be.

And this is where we came in. Sorry for the long intro, but I had to tell you about Tark. Speaking of my Orc boyfriend, he seemed to know something was wrong with me the minute he opened the front door.

"What's wrong, baby? What happened to make you so upset?" he asked, frowning at me.

"What makes you think I'm upset?" I said, trying to sound like I was fine—like I didn't care. I didn't want to look weak in front of him. I had this idea that if he knew what had happened at work, he might start to agree with my boss's assessment of me—that I was nothing but a weak-willed, fat, stupid, no good—

Okay, I had to stop thinking of myself like that. I knew for sure I wasn't stupid—it was just so hard to remember anything good about myself when all I heard at work was an endless stream of negatives.

Tark followed me into his house, insisting that he wanted to know what was wrong.

"I know when you're upset," he told me. "I can see it in your eyes and the way you hold yourself. Please, baby..." He knelt before me, getting down on my level, and took my shoulders in his hands. "Please, just *tell* me—was it that fucking boss of yours again?"

This time I couldn't deny it. I think the look of concern on his face was my final undoing. Suddenly, I couldn't hold the misery and shame inside any longer. Nodding my head, I felt my face crumple as the tears started.

"He...he said some things to me about...about m-my weight. Right in front of my c-coworkers," I whispered, the words coming out choppy because of my sobs.

Mr. Price had always yelled at me in private before—having him degrade me in front of Katrina and Jeremy felt like too much—more than I could bear.

Tark's face darkened.

"That fucker! I'll fucking kill him!"

"No, you c-can't!" I exclaimed though my sobs. "The police would start asking what...what happened to him. And an unhappy assistant would be a...a p-prime suspect!"

"Goddess damn it!" he growled and ran a hand through his hair. Then he took a deep breath and rose to his feet.

I was afraid at first that he was going to leave the house and go hunting for Mr. Price after all. Instead, he scooped me into his arms and went to sit on the couch.

I pressed my face to his chest as the sobs choked me. All of the pain and hurt and humiliation...I couldn't hold it inside anymore. It was too much...just *too much*.

Tark didn't say anything at first. He just rubbed my trembling back and shoulders soothingly with his big, warm hands and let me cry.

"It's okay, Babygirl," I heard him murmur at last. "It's okay—let it out. Just let it all out."

Somehow his acceptance of my grief and pain made it easier to do exactly that. I hadn't had anyone hold me while I cried since I was a little girl. I knew I was getting Tark's T-shirt soaked with tears, but he didn't seem to care. He just held me tight and let me cry.

At last the sobs tapered off and I began to feel better—though I was sure I looked like a mess. My eye make up was probably all smeared but I did feel more like myself.

"You okay, Babygirl?" Tark rumbled, looking down at me with concern in his golden eyes.

Hesitantly, I nodded.

"I…I think so. Better than I was, anyway."

"You want to talk about it?" he asked, raising his eyebrows.

I shook my head.

"It's just the same kind of thing—except this time instead of saying nasty things to me while we were alone, he did it in front of my coworkers. It was just really, really *humiliating*."

His face twisted.

"I hate that you have to go somewhere and be treated like that every day! What the fuck is wrong with humans, letting that happen to you?"

I sighed.

"I don't know. I told you—my boss is the CEO's brother so there's nothing I can do about it. And I can't quit—I'd owe over a hundred thousand dollars and I don't have that kind of money."

"Well you can't go on like this!" he protested.

I shook my head.

"Please—I don't want to talk about it. I'm almost halfway through school—if I can just make it for four more years I'll be a Pharmacist and then I'll be free."

"Will you, though?" he asked skeptically. "Be free, I mean. I thought you said you were still under contract to that human company even after you graduate."

"Only for two years," I said. "And I won't be working under Mr. Price then."

"But you'll still be working for a company that's letting you be abused," he pointed out. "How can you trust a place like that? A big corporation that doesn't give a fuck about their workers and only cares about profits?"

"I *don't*—not completely. But I really don't have any choice. I'm stuck here." I took a deep breath and swiped at my eyes. "Anyway, it helps to have you to talk to about it. Thank you for letting me cry and for not being judgmental about my choices or my, uh, curves."

"Ah, baby…" he sighed and placed a gentle kiss on my forehead. "How could I be judgmental when you're so fucking gorgeous?"

I gave a sad little laugh.

"Gorgeous…right. I'm a mess right now, I'm sure."

"You're a *little* messy," Tark acknowledged. Reaching between us, he raised the hem of his T-shirt, showing washboard abs, and used it to dab at my wet eyes. "But you're still gorgeous," he finished, smiling at me.

"You're so sweet to me." I sighed and snuggled against him. "I've never had anyone treat me like you do—not since I was little."

"You haven't? What about your aunt and uncle—the ones who raised you?" he asked, frowning. I had told him as little about my childhood as possible, so the fact that my aunt and uncle had raised me was pretty much the limit of his knowledge of my past. Well, other than the fact that my mom had died and my dad had left when I was young.

I shook my head.

"No, they didn't do this kind of thing. I mean, they didn't hug me like you do. They barely tolerated me, to tell the truth. I don't think they would have taken me in at all except they thought it wouldn't be 'Christian' to let me go into the foster care system and they were afraid their friends at church would talk about them if they did."

"Seriously?" He looked at me with a frown. "That's fucked up, sweetheart."

"I know." I hung my head. "I think that's why my boss's criticism and nastiness bothers me so much. He says the same kinds of things *they* used to say to me. About me being stupid and fat…"

But I couldn't finish—I was too ashamed. I shook my head and looked down at my hands.

"Hey, Babygirl, look at me." Gently, Tark raised my chin until our eyes met. "You're *beautiful,*" he murmured, stroking my cheek. "And you're fucking *brilliant* too. I didn't understand half of that stuff Madam Healer was telling you that first day we met but you soaked it up like a fucking sponge!"

"It's not that different from what I'm already studying," I pointed out.

"Which is *also* fucking hard to understand," Tark pointed out. He pushed my hair away from my face. "You know what your problem is? You've never had anyone to believe in you—anyone to baby you."

"Baby me?" I frowned uncertainly. "What do you mean?"

"I mean, someone to be sweet to you—to comfort you when you feel hurt. To be there for you, no matter what," he clarified.

I felt my heart give a little leap.

"I haven't had anything like that since my dad left when I was eight," I admitted in a low voice. "I mean, I haven't had anyone to hold me like you are now."

"Nobody at all?" he asked.

I shook my head.

"Not for years. I, uh, have this one memory of my dad holding me and kissing my knee—I skinned it learning to ride a bike, you know? And it *seemed* like he loved me. But not long after that, he left and never came back."

Tark frowned.

"It's fucked up that humans act like that. How could he just leave you?"

I shook my head.

"I don't know. Pretty much my whole childhood I used to imagine that he was going to come back for me someday and take me away from my aunt and uncle." I sighed. "But of course, that never happened. In fact, before I moved out my uncle told me that they'd contacted him after my mom died and he refused to come take me. So I guess he didn't love me, after all."

"Aw, Babygirl..." He pulled me close to him again, nestling the top of my head under his chin. "You don't have to feel like that anymore, you know."

"Feel like what?" I asked, snuggling against him. I have to admit, I loved our size difference. He made me feel so little...so cared for and loved.

"Like nobody loves you or cares about you." He pulled me closer and squeezed me in a tight hug. "Because *I* care about you—*I love you.* And I want to take care of you."

I felt as though the breath had caught in my throat. We had only been dating a few weeks at this point—it should have been too early to say those three little words. But it wasn't—it *so* wasn't. Hearing Tark say that to me seemed to heal something in my heart—something that had been broken since I was little. I felt my eyes welling up with tears again but this time they were tears of joy.

"What's wrong, sweetheart?" He looked down at me with worried golden eyes. "Should I not have said that? I'm sorry—I couldn't help it."

"No, no—it's not that." I sniffed and swiped at my eyes again. "I'm just crying because, well, because I love you *too*. And it's been so long since I could say that to anyone...or believe anyone who said it to me."

"Aw, baby..." Leaning down, he placed gentle kisses on my wet eyelashes, kissing away my tears.

"Oh, Tark..." I threw my arms around his neck and pressed my wet cheek to his rough, bristly one.

8

HARMONY

If you have a Daddy Kink, you can go read Chapters 8 (Page 121) and 9 (Page 124) in the Bonus Daddy Section. Then come back and continue reading the book at Chapter 10 (Page 70). If you don't have a Daddy Kink, just keep reading, you won't miss anything.

Being that close to him when I was feeling so many emotions—feeling so open and vulnerable with him—seemed to do something to my body. Pressing my face to his neck, I breathed him in and felt myself reacting to his wild, woodsy scent. My nipples were suddenly hard and between my thighs I felt wet and ready.

I rubbed against him, moaning softly as my tight nipples pressed against his broad chest. God, what was wrong with me? One minute I was bawling my eyes out and the next I was so horny I felt like I might crawl out of my skin!

Tark seemed to sense the shift in me because when he pulled back from our embrace to look at me, his golden eyes were half-lidded.

"Mmm, what's going on with you, Babygirl?" he murmured. "Feeling some kind of way, are you?"

"I might be," I admitted breathlessly. "Tark…I think…no, I know—I want to be naked with you."

His eyes blazed and then went lazy with lust and his voice dropped to a soft growl.

"I don't know if you're ready for that yet, baby."

"Yes, I am," I insisted. "I know we haven't been together that long but I trust you! And I want…no, I *need* to be close to you. With no clothes on."

"All right, but we're taking it slow," he said. "And we're not going further than I think you can handle."

Then he lifted me in his arms and carried me into the bedroom.

9

HARMONY

Tark lay me down gently on his enormous bed and I felt like a princess in a fairytale. He had a deep red coverlet that was made of some kind of extremely soft fur. It felt amazing against my cheek when I rubbed against it—I wondered how it would feel against my nude body.

I'll admit, I was a little shy to be naked in front of him—especially after hearing how "fat" I was from Mr. Price. But the curtains were drawn and the day outside was cloudy, which meant the bedroom was quite dim. So when Turk took off his shirt and then got on the bed with me, I started unbuttoning my blouse.

"No, wait—let me," he rumbled, putting one big hand on mine to stop me.

I looked up at him.

"You want to…"

"I want to undress you. Didn't I say I was going to take care of you, baby?" he asked.

"Yes." I nodded.

"Good, then let me do this."

He began unbuttoning the little pearl buttons on my blouse and as he did, he leaned forward and began laying hot, gentle kisses on my bare throat.

"*Ohhh*," I moaned as his hot, wet mouth traveled up and down my neck and then down to my chest, just above my breasts.

"Mmm, Babygirl, your skin tastes so sweet," he murmured as he slipped the blouse all the way off. "Are you ready to let me take off your bra now?"

"Yes…" I nodded. My breasts were actually a part of me I liked and Tark seemed to like them too.

"Gods, look at those sweet nipples," he growled softly as he helped me out of my bra. He cupped my right breast in his left hand and gently thumbed the nipple, making me squirm. "You like that, Babygirl? You want me to suck your sweet nipples for you?"

"Y-yes," I whispered breathlessly.

"Then ask me—ask me to do it," he urged, his voice rough with desire.

"Please, Tark—I want you to suck my nipples," I moaned, thrusting my breast further into his hand.

"Good girl—love to hear you ask me for what you want—what you *need*," he murmured. Then he bent his head over my chest and swirled his tongue lightly around my left nipple. At the same time, he was still tugging and teasing my right nipple with his fingers.

I gasped and arched my back—it felt so *good*. And I loved the way he was teasing me. His hot mouth on my sensitive peaks was driving me *crazy*.

Tark took his time, going back and forth and sucking each nipple in turn. Sometimes he teased me with his tongue and then he would suck my tight peak deep and hard, sending sparks of pleasure/pain from my sensitive tips straight to my pussy. I was getting so hot and wet by now that I didn't know how much more I could take.

"Please, Tark!" I begged breathlessly. "Please, I need *more*."

He sucked my nipple even harder for a moment, making me gasp, before finally looking up.

"Mmm, babygirl—what's wrong? Are you feeling all achy between your legs?" he rumbled.

Biting my lip, I nodded.

"Yes, I am. I want…I want more of you. And I want you to have more of me!"

Tark gave me a stern look.

"Tell me what you mean, baby—tell me what you want."

"I want…" I bit my lip and pressed my thighs together. "I want you to touch me," I confessed at last.

"Like this, you mean?" And he slid one big hand into the waistband of my skirt and cupped my pussy through my lace panties.

"*Ohhh*," I moaned softly and rubbed shamelessly against his fingers. "Yes, like that! Only even *more.*"

"Hmm, Babygirl—are you asking me to pet your soft little pussy without your panties on?"

I could feel my cheeks heating with a blush but the intent way he was looking at me made me feel like I *had* to answer.

"Yes," I said in a small voice. "I want…I need you to pet my bare pussy."

"Mmm, I'd be happy to do that for you, Babygirl. I'd love to pet my sweet baby's pussy," he growled. "But first let's get this off."

He removed my skirt, sliding it slowly down my legs. Now all I was wearing was my white lace panties. I felt a shiver of vulnerability go through me, but the way Tark was looking at me made me feel beautiful.

"Gods, baby—so fucking gorgeous," he growled hoarsely, looking me up and down. "Love your sweet little body! Come here."

And pulling me close, he fit me into the crook of his arm so that he was lying on his side and I was on my back with my head pillowed on one broad bicep.

"Now look at me while I touch you," he ordered, slipping his fingers beneath the waistband of my panties. "Look at me while I pet your soft little pussy."

As he spoke, I felt his long fingers parting the outer lips of my pussy. I gasped and jerked my hips as they slipped into my wet interior and found the aching button of my clit.

"Oh, did I find a sensitive spot?" Tark raised an eyebrow at me, grinning a little. "Does it feel good when I touch you there?"

"Yes!" I moaned as he began to circle my clit gently with one fingertip. "It feels…feels really *good.*"

"That's because you're being a good girl and spreading your sweet pussy for me," he growled softly. "Does it feel good when I pet you here?"

"It feels *so* good!" I moaned. "I…I think I might come soon."

His eyes went half-lidded and a deep growl that was pure lust came from his throat.

"Gods, Babygirl—you don't know how bad I want to make you come! But not like this."

And to my dismay, he pulled his long fingers out of my panties.

"Tark!" I nearly wailed. "What are you doing? I was so *close.*"

"But you need to get even closer, baby. Don't worry, I'm going to make you come. But not with my fingers."

And then he sat up, hooked his thumbs in the waistband of my panties, and pulled them all the way off.

"Oh, Tark!" I exclaimed. I felt suddenly shy, being completely nude like this. The red fur coverlet was incredibly soft against my bare skin as I rolled over to cover myself with my arms.

"No, baby…" Tark shook his head as he pushed me gently but firmly back onto my back. Then he put his hands on my knees and began pulling my legs apart.

"Oh! What are you doing?" I asked, biting my lip.

"I need you to open for me now, Babygirl," he said sternly.

I nibbled my lip some more.

"Why?" I asked softly.

"So I can taste you," he rumbled, his eyes blazing.

I felt an immediate surge of self-doubt. I'd never had a guy go down on me before.

"What…what if you don't like it, though?" I asked softly. "Like, what if you don't like the taste or the smell or…"

Tark silenced me by putting the two fingers he'd been using to stroke me earlier into his mouth. He sucked them, his golden eyes half-lidded as he looked at me. My heart was racing as he finally cleaned all my juices off his fingers and pulled them out of his mouth.

"Spread for me, Babygirl," he growled and it wasn't a request. "Let me eat that sweet little pussy."

Feeling like my heart might beat its way right out of my chest, I did as he ordered.

"Good girl. Goddess—look how wet you are!" he murmured as he got into position between my thighs. He was so big that his broad shoulders split me wide, making my pussy open even more for him.

I felt a rush of embarrassment laced with desire as he looked down at me. His face said he was looking at a rare treasure—one he'd been longing to own.

"Been wanting to do this from the first minute you ran into me out in the middle of Main Street," he growled, looking up at me. "Now spread nice and wide for me so I can taste that sweet pussy."

"All right," I murmured submissively. Seeing how much he wanted to do this definitely put me more at ease. I was still a little nervous about being so spread out for him, but not as uncertain as I had been before he reassured me.

"Mmm, baby…" he rumbled. Leaning forward, he rubbed one bristly cheek against the soft curls on my mound, making me moan and buck my hips.

Tark looked up at me, his eyes filled with lust.

"Sorry, Babygirl—was that too scratchy for you? Is your soft little pussy sensitive?"

"Yes, I…I think it is," I admitted breathlessly.

"I promise to be more gentle, then," he growled softly. "Like this…"

And leaning over again, he placed a hot, open-mouthed kiss directly on my open pussy.

I moaned and wiggled my hips as his tongue slid deep, caressing my clit as he kissed my pussy the same way he kissed my mouth.

"Oh, Tark!" I moaned. He was so big and strong he could have broken me in half without even trying but instead he was being so sweet to me—so gentle, just like he'd promised and I loved it!

I slid my fingers into his coarse black hair because I had to have something to hold on to as he continued to explore me. He was flicking my clit with the tip of his tongue and then I felt two long, thick fingers sliding inside me.

"Oh! Oh, Tark! Yes!" I gasped, arching my back and bucking my hips as his fingers filled me to the hilt. "Oh God, yes—just like that!"

Tark growled deep in his throat and redoubled his efforts. Sucking my clit into his mouth he began to tease and lick it over and over while at the same time he was fucking me with those thick fingers.

And then I felt something different—he wasn't just thrusting into me anymore, he was rubbing—rubbing the inner walls of my pussy. It felt like he had found another clit, there inside me. But the feelings he was giving me were even deeper and more primal and they were pushing me closer and closer to the edge of coming.

"Oh!" I moaned as the pleasure overtook me. "Oh, *Tark!* Oh, God, *yes!*"

I don't know what I was babbling, but I was pulling his hair and bucking my hips like a madwoman. I couldn't help myself—no one but me had ever made me come before and the feeling of being completely out of control while the pleasure soared through me was almost too much!

As the intense sensations went on and on, I felt something else inside me—something powerful uncurling—something that had perhaps lay dormant or sleeping all of my life felt like it was waking up. But what was it?

I didn't know and I couldn't analyze it—not when I was coming so hard. I didn't know how he was doing it but Tark seemed to be drawing out my orgasm, making it last somehow. My toes curled and my back arched...then I started seeing black spots dancing in front of my eyes.

"Oh!" I gasped. "Oh God, Tark...I can't...I think I'm going to... going to..."

But before I could get the words "I'm going to faint" out of my mouth, everything went black.

10

HARMONY

"Babygirl? Harmony? Are you all right?"

I woke to find Tark leaning over me, his golden eyes anxious. It reminded me of right after we'd first met when I had fainted from shock and pain.

Then I realized I must have fainted again. But how or why I had blacked out escaped me until I tried to move my legs and felt how sensitive I was between them.

"Ohhh, what happened to me?" I asked, blinking up at him. "The last thing I remember is you going down on me and then—"

I broke off abruptly as a second face appeared above my own. To my extreme embarrassment, it was Madam Healer.

"Oh, uh…" I scrambled to cover myself and was relieved to find that Tark had thrown the red fur coverlet over me. So though I was still naked beneath it, I was at least covered. Still, it was disconcerting to see someone I was beginning to think of as a teacher and a mentor leaning over me when I was in such a state.

"Please don't trouble yourself, Harmony. I'm only here to make certain you're all right," she said.

"Oh, er...I'm fine. I think," I said quickly, tugging the blanket a little higher. I wished I could just disappear beneath it and die quietly of embarrassment in peace!

"Sorry—I had to call her over. You really scared me, baby," Tark said. "First you fainted and then your skin was glowing all over!"

"It was?" I tried to think if I'd felt my skin doing anything weird, but I couldn't remember anything. Though I *did* have a vague memory of the feeling of something powerful waking up inside me. What had *that* been all about?

"You were—glowing all over the fucking place," Tark assured me earnestly. "So I called for Madam Healer. But by the time she got over here, the glowing had stopped."

"Er, how long was I out for?" I asked. "And why was I glowing?" I looked at Madam Healer to answer this last question, but she only shrugged her slim shoulders.

"I'm sorry, Harmony, but I don't know what could have caused the glow. My best guess would be that it has something to do with your magic."

"My magic?" Other than the strange test Goodie Albright had done on me my first day in Hidden Hollow and the fact that I could draw the magic doors that let me go back and forth between here and the Human Realm, I hadn't seen any signs of magical abilities yet.

"Yes, the more you come to Hidden Hollow, the more responsive it grows," Madam Healer said, nodding gravely.

"But...does this mean I'm going to er, get all glowy and faint every time I do anything, uh, intimate?" I asked anxiously. Tark already thought I was too fragile—if he was afraid I might faint every time I came, we would never get to go all the way!

She shook her head.

"I don't know—I don't think so. Tark told me you were in the throes of pleasure when the incident occurred. If I had to take a guess, I would think it was simply the intense pleasure coupled with the fact that you were being intimate with a magical being that called to your magic and caused it to manifest."

"But is it going to happen again? Like every time we, er…" I cleared my throat, unwilling to go on. But of course Madam Healer understood.

"No, I don't think it will happen every time," she said, obviously trying to be comforting. "You're just having growing pains—your magic has been in its infancy all this time and now that you've found Hidden Hollow, it's beginning to stretch and grow."

"Um…okay. But what good is it? I mean, I don't even know how to use it!"

"When the time comes, you will know," she said gravely. "Those with magic in their blood find that it rises to the occasion when they have need of it."

I nibbled my lower lip.

"Er, thank you, Madam Healer. I'm, uh, sorry you had to see me like this."

She gave her hissing laugh and her forked tongue flickered between her red lips.

"Please don't be embarrassed—as a Healer, I see people in all kinds predicaments. One incident in particular comes to mine—a Centaur and a Pixie tried to get together…oh, but I probably shouldn't tell that." She laughed again.

"What? But how?" I asked blankly. "I mean, Centaurs are as big as horses and Pixies are as tiny as hummingbirds—at least the ones I've seen."

"Oh, some growth magic for the Pixie was definitely involved," she assured me. "But they didn't use enough of it and she started shrinking again er, mid-copulation, if you will."

"That must have been a fucking mess!" Tark growled.

"Yes, it was. However, I *was* able to get them disentangled," Madam Healer said. "After that, they decided to just be good friends." She smiled. "Well, I really must be going now."

"Thank you for coming over," Tark said. He was wearing his jeans but his chest was still bare, I noticed. "I'll walk you to the door."

"No need—I can let myself out."

And Madam Healer nodded to us and slithered out the bedroom door.

11

HARMONY

As soon as she was gone, I looked up at Tark.

"Er...sorry for scaring you," I said weakly. "I didn't mean to faint."

"Of course you didn't, baby." He settled on the bed beside me and gathered me into his arms. "Goddess, I didn't know what to think! I was afraid I'd broken you somehow at first."

"I told you, I'm not that breakable!" I said crossly. "Just because *you're* huge doesn't make *me* tiny and weak. Most of the human men I know think I'm way too big—they don't want a plus-sized girl who's also as tall or taller than them."

"Well, you're tiny compared to me," he rumbled, stroking my hair gently. "I'll just have to be more careful with you from now on."

I groaned.

"That's what I was afraid of! Please don't think we can't, you know, have sex because of what just happened." I looked at him earnestly. "Because I really want to have sex with you—like a *lot.*"

Tark rumbled laughter.

"And I want to make love to you, too, Babygirl. But not right now."

"Why not?" I demanded. "I still have..." I looked at the time charm on my arm. "Two whole hours before I have to get back to work. That should be plenty of time."

"No, I'm not risking getting you overloaded again right away," Tark said firmly. "It's pretty fucking clear something is going on with your magic—we need to wait until it settles down before we do anything else."

"But we don't even know what it's doing or when it will be *done* doing it," I pointed out. "I don't want to live my life waiting on some weird thing inside me to finish whatever business it has before you and I really get together!"

To be honest, the intense orgasm he'd given me had made me hungry for more. I still felt hot and wet between my legs and I also wanted to see his equipment—which he had yet to show me. Not to mention I was extremely eager to feel it inside me.

But Tark wasn't backing down.

"No," he said firmly, frowning. "I'm *not* taking any more risks with you, Babygirl."

I sighed because I could tell he meant it. He could be very stern at times—maybe because he was so protective of me.

"Will you at least cuddle me then?" I asked in a small voice.

He rumbled laughter.

"What do you think I'm doing?" He nodded down to where his arms were around me and I was pressed against him.

"I meant *without* the blanket," I clarified, wiggling against him. "Please?"

"Well…all right."

"And could you take off your jeans, too—so we can cuddle naked?" I asked hopefully.

Tark shook his head but there was a spark of amusement in his golden eyes.

"Determined little thing, aren't you? No, baby, I'm not taking off my jeans. You're too damn tempting and holding you naked is only going to make it harder to resist you."

"All right," I sighed. At least he still had his shirt off, showing his mouthwatering bare chest. I would just have to be happy with what I could get.

Tark got up and I held open the blanket for him to climb in beside me. As soon as he did, he took me in his arms.

I sighed happily as I pressed against his big body and laid my head on his shoulder.

"Mmm, you're always so *warm*," I murmured as I breathed him in. His spicy, masculine scent was so comforting—he smelled like home, I thought.

"And you're so soft," he rumbled, stroking my hair. "Love you, Babygirl. I'm glad you're all right—you really had me worried for a while there."

"Sorry," I said and yawned. "Mmm, I'm sleepy now."

"Close your eyes and take a nap," Tark told me. "Don't worry—I'll wake you up in plenty of time to get back to work."

"Okay." I sighed deeply and let my eyelids drift closed. I had never fallen asleep with another person before—my two other brief encounters with men had been exactly that—brief. But with Tark, I felt safe and loved and cherished.

Yes, that was the word—*cherished,* I decided. That was exactly how he made me feel. Despite the awful time I'd had at work and the embarrassing encounter with Madam Healer, I still felt good. I felt happy because I knew instinctively I was safe in the arms of a male who would kill or die to protect me.

Those were my last thoughts as I finally drifted off.

I had no idea how soon my comforting bubble of safety would burst.

12

HARMONY

By the time I finally drew the magical doorway that led back to the ladies room in the Bentley Pharmaceuticals office, I was feeling calm and relaxed. I wasn't going to let Mr. Price get under my skin again, I told myself. He was just a spiteful, nasty man and who cared what he thought? I had Tark and he loved me and thought I was beautiful. That was enough for me.

I was so determined to let my boss's nasty comments roll off my back that he actually noticed it.

"What's wrong with you, Miss Ward?" he demanded, after he'd called me an 'idiot' for letting his coffee get cold and I didn't react. "You don't seem as sharp as usual—not that you're *ever* very sharp," he added. "You have the IQ of a slice of toast!"

"I aced Organic Chemistry," I said coolly. "I don't know many slices of toast that can do that."

"Well!" He looked at me, his pale eyes going wide with shock. "What's gotten into you? You're not the same since lunch."

"That's because I went home," I snapped. "And spent some time with decent people who care about me. Which is something I very much doubt you have—maybe that's why you're so nasty all the time."

I had gone too far—I knew it as soon as the words left my mouth. But I couldn't take them back—nor did I want to. I'd been a limp dishrag long enough, just soaking up my evil boss's abuse. It was high time I stood up for myself!

Mr. Price seemed so surprised by my words that he didn't know what to say or do at first.

"You...you'll regret that insubordination, Miss Ward!" he snapped. "How dare you speak to me like that?"

"How dare *you* speak to me the way you do?" I shot back. "You're always so hateful and cruel—it's like you *enjoy* being mean. Maybe you should see someone about that. Don't we have a mental wellness program at Bentley where you can meet with a therapist?"

"You...I..." Mr. Price didn't seem to know what to say. Finally, he fell back on an old standby. "I'll go see the therapist when *you* see a weight councilor or a dietician," he snapped. "Maybe when you lose some of that *blubber* you'll be marginally attractive."

"Nice try," I said flatly. "But it just so happens that I have someone in my life who loves me *just the way I am*. So I don't give a flying *fuck* what you think about my weight!"

I don't usually swear but I'd had enough of his abuse and I wasn't going to take it anymore!

Mr. Price's pale eyes narrowed in obvious frustration.

"I *thought* it must be something like that," he muttered, apparently speaking more to himself than to me. "Damn it!"

Then he turned on his heel and stormed out of the office.

I watched him go with a feeling of triumph. He couldn't hurt me anymore. Then a thought occurred to me—what if he was going to HR to get me fired?

The blaze of joy I'd felt at finally standing up to my awful boss cooled some at that idea. But then I lifted my chin. If they tried to fire me, I would complain to HR and anyone and everyone else I could find. I had Katrina and Jeremy as witnesses now—they could testify about how horribly Mr. Price treated me.

And if I had to, I could go around the company and get a lawyer. CEOs and highly placed executives weren't exactly popular right now—I was sure I could get a jury on my side if it came to that.

Also, no matter how bad things got, I now had a refuge to run to—a place where people liked me and cared about me. And I had Tark.

I comforted myself with thoughts of Hidden Hollow as I waited to see if I was fired. But the rest of the day passed peacefully since Mr. Price never came back. Nobody called me to HR either, so I gradually began to relax.

By the end of the day, I was feeling positive that everything was going to be all right. Maybe Mr. Price would leave me alone from now on, since he knew his mean words couldn't get to me anymore. Also, I was going to be able to see Tark again very soon—we had planned to have dinner that night. And I had every intention of trying to seduce him afterwards—I still wanted those naked cuddles!

At last it was five o'clock and nothing bad had happened. My heart was light as a feather when I walked out to the parking lot. My plan was to go home and get into the sexy lingerie set I had bought last week. I would put it on under my regular clothes before I drew the magic door and went back to Hidden Hollow. Then, after supper—or maybe even before—I would slip off my skirt and blouse, revealing the sexy red teddy I'd bought just to tease Tark with.

And then—how could he resist me? I loved the fact that he loved my body so much—it made me feel like a goddess, which was certainly different from how every other man in my life had always treated me. I was no longer just the skinny girls' fat friend—I was the one Tark wanted and I wanted him right back, I thought happily as I pressed the clicker to unlock my Honda. My Orc boyfriend was—

My thoughts were cut off abruptly when someone grabbed me from behind and something wet and cold was slapped over my mouth and nose.

"Hey!" I shouted—or tried to shout, anyway. But whoever had me was strong—much too strong for me to break free. And besides, something strange was happening—the cold wet thing on my mouth and nose smelled oddly sweet and I was beginning to feel woozy.

"That's right," a familiar voice crooned in my ear. "Breathe it in—take it deep into your lungs!"

"What...who...?" I tried to say but the arm around my waist tightened sharply, making me gasp in another breath of air through the damp cloth.

As the world around me began to go gray, I realized that I was in trouble.

I just didn't know how much.

13

HARMONY

What woke me was a pounding headache and sharp pains in my wrists and ankles.

"*Ohhhh*," I groaned and tried to move, only to find that I couldn't.

"Don't bother trying to get up, Miss Ward," a familiar voice snapped. "I've made certain you're not going anywhere."

I blinked my eyes and looked around. I was sitting slumped over in a sturdy wooden chair. Someone had zip-tied my wrists to the arms of the chair and my ankles also had zip-ties in them—they were fastened to the chair's thick wooden legs.

"What in the Hell?" I muttered. My brain still felt like it was full of fog and my head was throbbing.

"Not quite Hell, but close," the voice said.

I looked up at last to see who was speaking and was surprised to see Mr. Price standing there in front of me. We were in an empty apartment with no furniture and no air conditioner—I was already starting to sweat, I thought, feeling miserable.

"Mr. Price, what are you doing?" I asked, frowning up at him.

"Whatever I want, Miss Ward." He gave me an evil grin over the rims of his reading glasses. "Whatever gives me pleasure and satisfies my hunger."

"*What?*" As the fog in my brain began to clear, I began to feel panicky. It didn't help that when I moved my feet I heard an ominous rustle. Looking down, I saw that the chair I was sitting on was right in the middle of a large, clear sheet of plastic. "What the Hell are you talking about?" I demanded. "What is all this?"

"This, my dear Miss Ward, is the last thing you're ever going to see," he told me, grinning maliciously. "Because you're going to meet your end in this room—but *not* until I've had my fill."

I had no idea what he was talking about, but there was no way I was sitting there waiting to find out.

"Help! *Help!*" I screamed as loudly as I could. "Help, I've been kidnapped! Help me! *HELP!*"

Through it all, Mr. Price simply stood there watching me with that same smirking grin on his narrow face.

"Shout as long and as loudly as you want," he told me when I finally stopped, panting for breath. "This building is abandoned. Nobody can hear you and come to interfere with my fun."

"With your *fun?*" I was beginning to get a bad feeling—a *really* bad feeling in the pit of my stomach. "What are you talking about? Why… why did you bring me here?"

"You'll find out soon enough," he said. "Are you frightened yet? Because you *should* be." His long nose twitched and he leaned closer to me and inhaled deeply. "Ah yes—*now* I smell the terror. Good, good… more! It's *delicious!*"

"What?" I sounded like a broken record, but nothing he was saying was making sense to me. How could he smell and taste my fear?

He was right though—I *was* terrified. My heart was pounding and my palms were clammy with sweat. Why would he bring me to an abandoned building and tie me to a chair and put plastic on the floor like an episode of *Dexter* unless he meant to kill me? There was no way he was letting me go—I was trapped here and I couldn't get loose!

Just as all this was racing through my head, I noticed something strange. There was a line of what looked like nearly invisible vapor flowing from me—right from the center of my body. And it was drifting up towards Mr. Price. Not drifting, exactly—he had his mouth open and it almost looked like he was *sucking* it out of me.

*Oh my God—he **is** sucking it out of me—is that the terror he was talking about?*

It was so weird and also scary. But it would have been scarier if I hadn't spent that last three weeks going back and forth to Hidden Hollow. By now, I was beginning to recognize magic when I saw it.

"Ahh, so tasty!" Mr. Price said, smacking his thin lips.

"What are you doing to me?" I demanded. "And how the Hell are you doing it?"

"What? Feeding on your emotions? Quite easily, Miss Ward—you see, it's my nature to feast on the negative emotions of others. And up until recently, yours were quite tasty and nourishing." He scowled. "Until you fell *in love.*"

He spat the words like they tasted nasty and he wanted to get them out of his mouth.

I shook my head.

"I don't understand."

"Of course you don't. Never fear, we have time so I will explain. You see, I'm a special kind of Creature I'm sure you've never heard of. I live by extracting pain, fear, sorrow, shame—all those tasty negative feelings—from humans like yourself. And for ages, you've been my main meal ticket! All the sorrow you felt every time I was cruel to you…all the anger you suppressed…and most of all, the delicious *shame* that overcame you every time I pointed out your weight issues." He made a smacking sound with his thin lips. "Delectable! Shame is my *favorite!*"

"Oh my God, you're a Sin Sucker!" I exclaimed, remembering the term Tark had used.

Mr. Price lifted his eyebrows in obvious surprise.

"So you *have* heard of my kind. How very strange."

"Not as strange as you might think," I said through gritted teeth. I was still scared but I was beginning to get mad too. So all this time he had been *feeding* on me? Sucking up the negative emotions he caused by belittling me and putting me down? What an asshole!

I squeezed my hands into fists. I was beginning to feel some tingling in my fingers—probably because my hands were going numb from the tight zip-ties.

"Ah yes—anger too! It's not as tasty as shame or pain or fear but it's still quite delectable!" Mr. Price—if that was even his name—pursed his thin lips and began inhaling again—sucking up my negative emotions like they were a rare treat.

"Hey—stop that!" I struggled to get free, even though I knew it was useless. "Let me go and leave me alone, you freak!"

"Now *that* is not very nice language, is it?" Mr. Price frowned at me. "Also, I think I'm tired of anger—it's too spicy for my palate. How about we try some more *fear?*"

As he spoke, something happened…he began to change. The business suit he was wearing began to stretch and lose the texture of fabric and the gray color of his jacket and pants spread to his face and hands.

At the same time, his narrow face started distorting itself. His nose became much sharper and longer and his narrow lips spread to reveal rows of razor-sharp teeth. His thinning hair disappeared altogether, absorbed into his scalp which was now gray as well. And his hands…his hands were now claws—each finger tipped in a razor-sharp point that looked capable of slicing my throat with no effort at all.

But it was his eyes that were the worst. The watery pale blue irises disappeared as a thick black film covered them. It covered the whites of his eyes too until they were nothing but two flat, black, obsidian voids staring at me.

Shark's eyes, I thought, feeling sick. *Predator's eyes*. There could be no reasoning with a monster that had eyes like that. Because Mr. Price—or whatever his real name was—had no pity in him. No remorse, no mercy or sympathy.

There was only hunger in that flat, black gaze and it was all centered on me.

"Yes…fear! How I *love* it!" The narrow lips parted again, revealing his jagged teeth and he inhaled deeply, sucking the nearly invisible vapor of terror from the center of my chest.

I was so scared I was afraid I might start crying and I knew if I broke down, I wasn't going to be able to defend myself. But defend myself how? I was zip-tied to the chair and the ties were so tight my fingers were going numb. Or at least, they were tingling even more than they had been. In fact, the tingles had become almost painful.

I spared a moment from staring in terror at the monster my boss had become to glance down at my fingers. To my surprise, they were *glowing.*

What the Hell? I thought, looking at myself. What was going on with me?

I remembered that Tark had said I was glowing after I had passed out earlier. And how Madam Healer thought it had something to do with my magic. She had also said that I would find my magic when I needed it.

Well, I needed it now!

I twisted my wrists desperately, not caring that the plastic zip-ties were digging into my flesh. My fingers started tingling even more—in fact, it felt like they were getting *hot.* Experimentally, I twisted my right hand under and managed to get my fingertip to touch the thin cord of plastic binding my wrist to the chair's arm.

I heard a thin sizzling sound and then the smell of burning plastic wafted up to my nose. What the Hell? Had my fingers gotten hot enough to *melt plastic?*

I didn't have much time to marvel at my new magical skill—whatever it was—though. Because Mr. Price was coming towards me.

"Let's see now, how about a little *bite?*" he asked, grinning at me to show those jagged teeth. "I like the taste of emotional pain but physical pain is extremely tasty too!"

He was getting closer and closer, shoving his face into mine. His breath smelled like death—I mean that. It smelled like something rotten and decayed and unspeakably foul. It made my stomach turn with revulsion.

"Disgust tastes nice too!" he snarled at me and then he was opening his mouth to take a bite of my shoulder.

As the points of his teeth grazed my arm, I yanked back and felt my right hand come free. Instinctively, I shoved it into his face to push him away. As I made contact with his gray skin, the dull golden-red glow that was emanating from my fingers abruptly brightened to a blinding radiance.

"Ahh!" Mr. Price's flat black eyes narrowed in pain and he seemed to want to get away from me, but he couldn't. It was like my hand was a powerful magnet and his face was made of iron.

Iron, I thought randomly. *But my hand is glowing gold…*

No sooner had the thought entered my head than something strange began to happen—(yes, even stranger than my glowing hand trapping my ex-boss who was also a Sin Sucker monster in place.)

Mr. Price began to change. His gray skin began to glow and then turn shiny and golden. At the same time, the part that had become gold —which was basically the whole left side of his face—seemed to freeze in place.

"Noooo!" he howled but already the bottom part of his jaw was going gold as well. "Nnnnnn!" His tongue was gold—I could see it. He raised his right arm and slashed at me.

I gasped and jerked my hand off his face, twisting away instinctively. I felt the tips of his claws graze my shoulder, slashing easily through the silk fabric of my work blouse and scratching my skin.

Unfortunately, when I stopped touching him, the engoldening effect—or whatever you want to call it—seemed to start reversing itself.

"Wha di' ya do ta me?" he howled, his tongue still half-frozen but beginning to "thaw" and turn back to the grayish-black color it had been before. "Wha di' ya *do?*"

He was fumbling with the golden side of his head—it really did look like a golden statue. And it must have been as heavy as gold too, because his neck couldn't support it and he was slumped over to one side.

While he was distracted with his new affliction, I desperately tried to free my other wrist and my ankles. But now that I was trying *consciously* to make my magic work, I found that it wouldn't anymore. The glow had faded and my fingers had turned back to regular digits again. No matter how much I yanked and tugged at the other three zip-ties, they didn't melt and nothing else happened either.

"I'll kill you!" the Mr. Price monster screamed at me. His tongue was completely unfrozen now and the left side of his head was rapidly going from gold to gray too. "I'll kill you, you little slut!"

He lunged at me and I twisted away so violently the chair toppled over.

"Oof!" I gasped as I made contact with the hard floor under the shiny sheet of plastic. I was on my left side with only my right arm free. Frantically I tried to unfasten the zip-tie on my left wrist, but I couldn't even reach it.

It was then that I heard a pounding on the door.

Thud…thud…thud!

"Harmony? *Harmony!*" a deep, familiar voice was shouting.

It was Tark! Relief flooded me. I had no idea how the big Orc had found me but I was so, *so* glad that he had.

"In here!" I wheezed—the breath had been knocked out of me by the fall. "In…*here!*"

But Tark wasn't inside yet and Mr. Price had nearly returned to normal now.

"Is that your 'true love'—perhaps even your Heartmate?" he asked, leering down at me. "Is he the one who likes you 'just the way you are'?"

"Yes, he is!" I spat at him, as furious as I was frightened.

"Then he must truly love you! Think how tasty his pain will be when he comes in and finds you *dead!*"

He lunged for me again and wrapped long, taloned fingers around my throat. But just then with a massive *THUD!* the door crashed open and Tark was there.

14

HARMONY

The big Orc was bare-chested and his golden eyes were wild. In his hands was a massive war ax—almost as tall as he was himself—with a blade as big as his torso.

Only someone as huge as Tark could have wielded such a weapon and let me tell you, he came in swinging.

"Stop!" Mr. Price squeezed my throat until I gasped and choked. "Come a step nearer and she dies!"

I saw Tark's eyes widen but he stopped in mid-swing. Gripping the axe handle so tightly his knuckles went white, he glared at my boss.

"Take your fucking hands off my woman!" he growled. "Unless you have a fucking death wish!"

"I don't think so." The Mr. Price Monster gave him a smug smile—if a shark can look smug, that is. "This little slut was my assistant long before she was your girlfriend—she belongs to *me*."

"The fuck she does!" Tark's voice came out in a menacing roar. "*Let her go!*"

"No," the Mr. Price Monster said coolly. "My, my—your rage is *so* delicious. And the way you feel so protective of her—*lovely*."

"You Sin Sucking bastard," Tark snarled. "Surely you know the minute you kill her, you're dead too!"

"That's only if you can catch me. Besides, I'm not going to kill her—I think I'll take her with me," Mr. Price told him. "I thought—"

But what he thought was something we never got to hear. Because at that moment, my fingers started tingling and glowing again.

I didn't hesitate—reaching up, I clamped my hand over the monstrous one that was closed around my throat.

"What? *Ahhh!*" the Mr. Price Monster screamed.

I could feel the power rushing through me—the mysterious energy that somehow changed what I touched. And this time, I did my best to direct it.

Faster! I thought at it. *Faster—more!*

My internal directions seemed to work because the hand wrapped around my throat was turning to gold *fast*—too fast for Mr. Price to squeeze my throat and kill me, thank goodness.

"No—*no!*" he roared and grabbed at his right arm—which was rapidly turning to either gold or a metal that looked like gold—and tried to pull it free.

He wasn't successful—his long curving claws had wrapped almost all the way around my throat and they weren't coming loose. But the momentary distraction was all the opening Tark needed.

With a deafening roar, he rushed forward and swung his axe just once, lopping off my boss's head as neatly as man might swing a golf club. Mr. Price's head went flying in a gout of black blood that spurted from the stump of his neck and then oozed all over the place.

His body remained in place for a second, then it crumpled to the ground, one long, golden hand still wrapped around my throat.

Tark was kneeling by me at once.

"Harmony? Baby?" he asked anxiously. "Are you okay? Please say you're okay!"

"Get it off me!" I was yanking at the golden arm with my one free hand. "Please—get it off!"

"Stop touching it," Tark said, frowning. "I think you're the one that's doing that—you're turning him to gold, somehow."

Indeed, the dead body of my old boss was continuing to turn to gold, right before my eyes. I realized that I was still clutching as the monstrous hand around my throat and yanked my hand away.

But it didn't seem to help. No more of Mr. Price's body turned to gold…but the golden part didn't turn back to flesh either. I waited for a moment, hoping it would change but it just wouldn't.

So there I was, lying on my side on the ground, still zip-tied to the chair by one wrist and both ankles, facing the dead body of a monster with a golden arm which was locked around my throat.

I can't deny, I started to lose it.

"Please, get me out of here! Get it off of me! *Please!*" I begged Tark.

"I'm trying, Babygirl!" He did his best to pry the golden fingers from around my neck, but they were fused together and even he couldn't break the solid bar of gold they had become. He tried, but he couldn't get his own fingers between them and my throat without choking me.

At last he had to resort to chopping the arm off with his axe, just above the elbow which was where the gold part ended when I had let go of it to stop my magic. Then, kneeling beside me, he drew a knife out of his boot and quickly cut the zip-ties that held me to the chair.

I tried to sit up but the golden arm hanging from my throat was incredibly heavy. It was literally like trying to lift myself with an anchor tied around my neck.

"Here, baby—I've got you." Slinging his axe over his back, Tark lifted me in his arms and carried me—golden arm and all—out of the abandoned apartment.

15

HARMONY

"How did you know where to find me?" I asked, when I had finished crying. Because yes, I shed some tears—I'd just been through a near-death experience and it wasn't quite over yet. Not until I got the damn golden arm off of my neck. It felt like some grisly necklace and it was extremely heavy lying on my chest and abdomen as it was.

"I had a feeling about an hour ago that something wasn't right with you," Tark rumbled, looking down at me. He had carried me through the whole building, going down several flights of stairs since there was no power and the elevator didn't work. It gave me a whole new appreciation of his strength because I swear the damn golden arm weighed as much as I did!

"You...had a feeling? But why?" I asked, looking up at him.

"Dunno." He shrugged. "Maybe because of your magic coming out while I was, you know, making you come. It formed some kind of connection between us. Anyway, I just *knew* you were in trouble. I went to Goodie Albright right away and asked her to make me a finding spell and then draw a door. She was able to get me in the same basic area as you—I just didn't know which apartment you were in until I heard you shouting."

"I'm *so* glad you came for me!" I nuzzled my cheek against him—as well as I could with the damn arm in the way. "He would have killed me otherwise!"

"I don't think so—you nearly killed him yourself before I swung my axe," he objected. "That's some powerful magic you've got there, Babygirl."

"I don't even know what it is," I admitted, looking down at the arm again. "It just *happened* when he tried to hurt me."

"Looks to me like he *did* hurt you." Tark frowned at my ripped blouse and the scratches on my shoulder and cheek. "I should have gotten to you sooner."

"The fact that you were able to tell I was in trouble and come at all is amazing," I told him. "I'll heal—I just have to get this horrible arm off me!"

"I think maybe Madam Healer can help with that. Or if not, we'll ask Goodie Albright. Somebody must have a spell or a potion that will do the trick. And look—here we are."

He carried me outside as he talked and I saw a magic door, standing in the overgrown parking lot just outside the abandoned apartment building.

"Thank God!" I said fervently.

"No, thank the Goddess," Tark corrected me. "It's her power that makes Hidden Hollow and all the Creatures that live there possible. But we can talk about that later. For now, let's get you out of here."

And then, much to my relief, he carried me out of the Mortal Realm and back to Hidden Hollow.

16

HARMONY

"Well, I think we know what your magic is all about now," Madam Healer said as she carefully poured the bright blue potion she'd concocted over the golden fingers locked around my neck.

"What?" I asked. I was feeling more than a little claustrophobic. I normally don't even like to wear a choker necklace because it makes me feel like I can't breathe and the golden monster fingers were squeezing me tight enough to make me *really* uncomfortable.

"Why, you're an alchemist, my dear," she said. "In the literal sense. You can turn base metals into gold."

"But Mr. Price wasn't made of metal," I protested, frowning.

"Actually, if he really was a Soul Sucker, he might have been—at least in part," she told me. "They're a kind of demon—spawned in the deep, dark places of the Earth. They have no mother or father—they're sentient rock that comes to life when evil touches it." She shrugged. "So it seems logical to assume that your Mr. Price must have had a lot of iron ore in his make-up."

"So…he was just a living demonic rock?" I asked doubtfully.

"Essentially." She nodded. "That's one reason you can't reason or plead with a Sin Sucker—they have no soul and their hearts, if they have one, are as hard as…well, as a rock. That's why they crave emotions."

"Well the bastard certainly got plenty of *my* emotions in the time I was working for him," I muttered. Then I had another thought. "So… do you think that was the *real* Mr. Price?"

"Almost certainly not," Madam Healer said, shaking her head. "If I had to guess, I would say the real Mr. Price is dead and buried somewhere and has been for a long time."

"Sin Suckers can mold themselves into any form they want," Tark said.

"Yes, they can," Madam Healer agreed. "He probably saw the real Mr. Price and realized he had power over others—which is the first ingredient in causing the formation of negative emotions."

I tried to feel bad for the real Mr. Price…and couldn't quite manage it. Nobody at work seemed to think that he had changed or was acting different in any way from the Sin Sucker that had taken his place, so it stood to reason that he'd probably been a piece of work too.

"I believe I have it softened enough now," Madam Healer said. "Tark, could you please try bending the fingers away from Harmony's neck?"

Tark did as she said and this time, much to my relief, he was able to open the long fingers enough to slip the hand from around my throat.

"Thank you!" I took a long, deep breath and then another. It felt so *good* to be able to do that again—and to have the heavy weight that had been resting on me for the past half-hour off my chest.

"You're welcome, my dear." Madam Healer smiled as Tark laid the golden arm down on the exam table beside me with a *clunk*. "And I'm glad you discovered your magic in time for it to save you."

"I did, but what good is it?" I asked. "I mean, other than the obvious, I guess—turning any other kind of metal to gold."

"Yes, you could be wealthy beyond your wildest dreams, if you used your magic that way," Madam Healer said thoughtfully. "*Or* you could turn your attention to other areas."

"Other areas? What other areas?" I asked, frowning.

"Well, a natural alchemist like you should also have an innate talent for brewing any kind of potion or healing elixir she turns her hand to," Madam Healer explained. "You'll know instinctively which ingredients go together and which would cause a dangerous reaction. That kind of medical intuition is absolutely *priceless*."

"Really?" I felt a little jolt of excitement. "That sounds amazing!"

"It's certainly something to think about," she said. "And if you'd like, I would be happy to teach you. Not that you'll need much teaching now that your talent has awakened—things will come to you naturally, I expect."

"Thank you!" I said, smiling at her. "I'd love to learn to brew potions and spells!" All the lessons I'd had from her so far had been fascinating—much more interesting than the boring regular chemistry I'd learned in the Human Realm.

Madam Healer gave me a pleased smile.

"Very well. Come see me tomorrow and we'll talk about it some more. But for now, let me give you a pot of healing salve and send you back home with Tark." She smiled at the big Orc. "I know he's longing to take care of you."

Tark's cheeks went dark green with a blush but he didn't deny it.

"I do need to get her home," he rumbled, nodding. "She's been through a lot today."

"She certainly has," Madam Healer agreed. "Here."

She pressed a tiny pot of salve into Tark's big hand and smiled.

I started to get off the exam table, but Tark was too quick for me. He swept me up into his arms and held me close to his broad chest.

"Come on, Babygirl," he rumbled. "Let's take you home."

17

HARMONY

At this point if you have a Daddy kink, go read Chapters 17 (Page 131), 18 (Page 134), and 19 (Page 138) in the Bonus Daddy section. Then go back to Chapter 20 (Page 114) to finish the book. If you don't have a Daddy kink, just keep reading as usual. ;)

As soon as we got back to his house, Tark insisted on running me a bath in his enormous bathtub.

"I'm honestly all right. I don't need a bath," I protested as I sank in up to my neck. "Ooo—ouch!" I added, because my cuts were stinging.

"You were saying?" Tark raised one sardonic eyebrow at me as he wetted a sponge and began to gently scrub me.

"Hey, it's just because the hot water stings," I said defensively.

"Exactly—it stings because you were scratched by a demon—a Sin Sucker," he said firmly. "We have to get those cuts *completely* clean before I put the healing salve on."

"Why?" I asked nervously. "Will they make me sick? Give me blood poisoning?"

"Worse—they could give you *soul* poisoning if we're not careful," he said grimly. "And you don't want that—the evil that was in the monster that attacked you could reach your heart and turn it as hard and cold as his was."

"No, I definitely don't want that!" I shivered. The thought of becoming like Mr. Price chilled me, even though I was neck deep in hot, soapy water.

"Of course you don't. Don't worry, baby—we're going to get you squeaky clean tonight," he promised. "Just let me wash you."

He took his time, scrubbing me all over—and I do mean *all* over. He ran his big hands all over my body until I was practically trembling with need. But though he took the time to tug my nipples and to scrub between my legs—which mostly consisted of him teasing my aching clit with his fingertip—he never quite let me come.

At last I was panting with desire.

"Please, Tark!" I begged. "Please, I need you!"

"Need you too, baby," he growled softly. "You think you're all clean now?"

"All clean and ready for naked cuddles," I assured him. "And this time I want you to get naked too!"

Tark gave me an uncertain look.

"I still don't know if you're ready for that, Babygirl. Remember I told you that Orcs have different, uh, equipment down there?"

"What, do you have a nest of tentacles or something?" I demanded, feeling thoroughly exasperated.

He rumbled a laugh.

"Hardly! I'm not a fucking Kraken, you know."

"Well, whatever you have, I want to see it," I said bossily. "And more than that, I want to *use* it. I nearly died today, you know. And if I had, I would have gone without ever getting to get really close to you."

"Aw, Babygirl—please don't talk like that!" His golden eyes were suddenly suspiciously shiny.

"Well, it's true," I pointed out. I sighed. "Look, I know you think I'm too small to, you know, take you, but at least let me try. I have some pretty big toys back home, you know."

His eyes were suddenly lazy with lust.

"Toys, is it? Hmm, why is this the first I'm hearing about them?"

I bit my lip, my cheeks feeling hot.

"Well…I mean, it's kind of embarrassing. But I wanted you to know that I can take you."

"You probably will be able to if I taste you first," he rumbled. "The question is, will you want to once you see what I've got in my pants?"

"What in the *world* do you have?" I demanded—I was extremely curious. "Come on, you *have* to show me."

Tark sighed.

"Well… I guess. But it's different from what human males have."

"Tark…" I put my hand on his arm and looked into his eyes. "Whatever it is, I want it," I told him. "You love and accept me just the way I am—what makes you think I can't do the same for you?"

"I just don't want to scare you off," he said in a low voice.

"You won't," I assured him. "I'm not going anywhere."

"All right, Babygirl—you asked for it." He had been kneeling by the tub but now he rose and held open a fluffy blue towel for me. "Come on—let's get you all dried off and then you can see what I've got for you."

18

HARMONY

Tark finished drying me off and then swung me into his arms and carried me into the bedroom. The minute he put me down in the center of his huge bed, I was reaching for him.

"Come here—cuddle me!" I demanded. "But first take off your jeans!"

He did as I asked, but I noticed that he left his underwear—which were black boxer-briefs—on. I started to protest, but he shook his head.

"No, baby—let me at least get you ready first. Then you can decide if you like what you see of not."

"Get me ready? How?" I asked frowning as he climbed on the bed with me.

"Like this," he growled. And reaching for me, he wrapped his massive hands around my waist and lifted me.

"Oh, Tark! What…what are you doing?" I gasped, but I had my answer soon enough. He was lying flat on his back and positioning himself so that I was straddling his head.

"There," he growled, looking up at me with half-lidded eyes. "Now we're ready."

"Ready for what?" I squeaked.

"Ready for this, Babygirl." And tugging on my hips, he pulled me lower until my pussy was positioned right over his mouth.

"Oh…oh, Tark!" I gasped. "Don't—I'll smother you!"

He gave a hungry laugh.

"Then fucking smother me, baby. I can't think of a better way to go!" His eyes roved over my body and went half-lidded. "Goddess, look at that soft little pussy, just begging to be tasted! Can't wait to feel you coming on my tongue."

"I mean it," I protested, still resisting as he tugged on my hips. "I'll crush you!"

He barked another laugh.

"Have you seen how big I am, baby? There's no way you can crush me with your soft, curvy little body. Now come on—if you want a look at what I have down below, I need to taste you first. Just in case one thing leads to another."

I wasn't sure what he was talking about, but I finally allowed him to tug me down until my pussy was in contact with his mouth.

I heard a low growl of approval and then I moaned in surprised pleasure as his warm, wet tongue invaded me. Leaning forward, I gripped the top of the headboard, trying to keep my balance as he began licking me in earnest.

"Oh…*ohhh!*" I heard myself moaning as I felt his tongue sliding deep inside me and then swiping up to tease my aching clit.

At first I tried to grip the top of the brass headboard and keep myself from putting too much pressure on him, but Tark wasn't having that. With a low, possessive growl, he gripped my hips even tighter and brought me down, insisting that I sit fully on his face without holding back.

I probably would have killed a human man that way, but a full-blooded Orc is a whole different kind of male. Tark seemed to be having no difficulty at all handling my weight—in fact, he seemed to love it. He was making low, hungry growling sounds as he ate me and I began to feel more free when I realized how much he was enjoying himself.

Gripping the top railing of the brass headboard harder, I began to ride him—pressing my pussy fully against his mouth. Somehow he managed to keep from cutting me with his tusks, though I could feel them bracketing my pussy as I rubbed against him.

My pleasure was already building and I began to get nervous when I realized how close I was to coming. Was I going to faint again? I thought I could feel a faint tingling in my fingertips but when I looked at them, I couldn't tell if they were glowing or not.

I would have stopped the big Orc if I could have, but by that time Tark was completely unstoppable. His long fingers were curled around my waist and his tongue was lashing me, teasing my swollen clit until I couldn't help myself anymore.

"Oh....oh, Tark!"

Suddenly, I was coming—coming so hard I was seeing stars flashing in front of my eyes. I gasped and rubbed myself against his wet tongue shamelessly as I gripped the headboard even tighter. Oh God, it felt so good...so *fucking good!*

I felt power running through my body as I went rigid with pleasure, my toes curling and my back arching. What was happening? What was I doing?

But when I finally opened my eyes, feeling apprehensive to see what my magic might have done, nothing looked different. The shiny brass headboard was still the same as far as I could see and Tark seemed fine—though he showed no signs of stopping.

"Tark, please!" I moaned, trying to pull away as his tongue lashed my overly sensitive clit again. "I need a minute before you make me come again!"

He finally heard me because he loosened his grip on my hips and I was able to pull away from his mouth. When I looked down at him, his eyes were blazing and his lips were wet with my juices.

"Gods, Babygirl—fucking love the way your soft little pussy tastes!" he growled.

"I can tell." I gave a shaky laugh. "But it's my turn now. You promised if I let you, er, taste me, that you'd let me see your equipment."

"Oh, right. Well…okay. But don't blame me if it scares you."

And with those cryptic words, he lifted me away from his face and tucked me into the crook of his arm instead.

19

HARMONY

I couldn't help noticing that there was an extremely large tent in the stretchy black material of his boxer-briefs. It drew me like a magnet and I reached for him at once.

"Easy, Babygirl," he rumbled, putting a hand over mine. "I know you're eager for your prize, but let's go slow."

"I'm tired of going slow!" I protested. "Let me see it!"

"All right…you asked for it."

With a sigh, he peeled down the waistband of his boxer-briefs revealing…

"Oh my God," I said blankly. "You've got *two* of them."

"All Orcs do," Tark told me.

I stared in surprise at the two shafts that had been revealed when he pulled down his shorts. One of them—the bottom one—was absolutely massive. It was even bigger than my biggest toy, I thought as apprehension raced through me. Topped with a broad, flaring crown, it had a shaft so thick I didn't think I could even fit my fingers around it, let alone fit it in my pussy! It was also covered with parallel lines—raised ridges that ran the entire length of it on both the top and bottom sides.

The second shaft was situated directly above the larger one. It was considerably smaller, though still a good size. It was also shorter. At least there was only one set of balls, I thought. They were massive and located right under the larger shaft.

It was surprising, I'll admit. But no matter how daunting the situation was, I wasn't giving up! I wanted to make love with Tark—I wanted him inside me.

"Okay, tell me all about this," I said and reached out to take the smaller shaft in my hand. "How does it work? Am I supposed to ride the smaller one first and then try the bigger one?"

"Actually, that's a good idea. Gods, your soft little hands feel good on me!" he groaned. "The top shaft—my secondary shaft—makes a special cum that helps you open for my bottom shaft. It also rubs against your clit and makes it swell and become more sensitive—that way you can come again when I fuck you."

"Mmm, I like that idea," I told him.

"Then climb on board, Babygirl," he growled. "Let me just get settled here…" He propped some pillows against the headboard and then motioned for me. "Come here and let me fuck you."

His dirty words made me feel hot all over again. I straddled his lap eagerly and rubbed the head of the smaller shaft against my open pussy. At once a warming precum started flowing from its tip. As I rubbed it against me, I could feel my clit swelling and getting even more sensitive.

"Oh!" I exclaimed, looking down at myself. My pussy was open and wet and I was aching inside—as though I needed to be filled.

"That's right, Babygirl—Gods, look at how hot and wet your soft little pussy is," Tark growled. "Just lower yourself down on my upper shaft—need to come in you with the top shaft in order to help you open for the bottom one."

Moaning softly, I did as he said. I could feel the second, larger shaft rubbing against my behind as I leaned forward and lowered myself down on the top one.

Even though it was smaller than the bottom shaft, it was still big enough to fill me and stretch my inner walls—which was exactly what I felt like I needed. I wiggled as I felt it slip all the way inside, the head pressing against the end of my channel.

"That's right, Babygirl," Tark growled softly. "Now just wait a minute…Gods!" He stifled a groan and then I felt something hot and wet spurting deep inside me. Was this the special cum that would help me take his larger lower shaft? It must be, I decided.

"Oh, Tark!" I moaned. "I can feel you coming in me—it feels so good!"

"Feels fucking good to me too, Babygirl," he groaned. "Gods your soft little pussy feels so good around me!"

He filled me completely with his cream until it was leaking out even with his smaller shaft fully inside me. When he finally pulled out, I could feel it gushing everywhere. It even slid down and coated my rosebud, making me tingle all over.

"Oh my God—we made a mess!" I said, looking down.

"That's all right," Tark assured me. "As long as it gets everywhere. Because now you have a choice, Babygirl."

"A choice?" I asked, raising my eyebrows. "What choice?"

"You get to pick how you want me to fuck you," he growled softly. Cupping my cheek he looked into my eyes. "We can just do it this way, with you facing me. My larger shaft goes into your pussy and my smaller shaft keeps rubbing against your clit to make you come."

"I like the idea of that," I purred. Though I had enjoyed having his smaller shaft inside me, I was dying to feel the much larger one stretching me out.

"Or…" He held up a finger. "You can choose the other way—it's what we Orcs call 'double fucking' and we only use it when we want to bind a woman-a Heartmate—to us forever."

"Forever?" I asked, my heart leaping in my chest. "Tark, do you really think—"

"I don't just think—I *know*, Babygirl," he said firmly. He stroked my cheek. "I know I want to be with you always—to be your mate forever. You're my Heartmate—the one I was always meant to be with. And I'm sure I'm your Heartmate, too. The question is, do you want to stay together and be Sworn to me for the rest of our lives?"

I didn't hesitate a minute.

"Yes!" Leaning forward, I threw my arms around his neck and nuzzled against him. "Yes, that's exactly what I want! But how do we do it?"

"Well, it might be a little challenging for you since you're so little," he rumbled. "But if you think you can take it, we'll try it."

"Try what?" I asked, pulling back to look at him. "What are we going to be doing? Or I guess I should ask, *how* are we going to be doing it?"

"You have to take both my shafts at once," he explained. "The larger one in your pussy and the smaller one in your tight little rosebud." He gave me a serious look. "Do you think you can do that for me, baby? Do you think you can take both of my shafts inside you at once?"

I bit my lip, thinking it over. On one hand, my ass was a sensitive area—though I had a lot of toys, I hadn't used many of them there. And while Tark's smaller shaft was considerably less girthy than the big one, it was still enough that I could really feel it opening my pussy. How would it feel in my ass—especially if I was getting skewered by the other, much more massive cock at the same time?

But on the other hand, I wanted to be Sworn to him as his Heartmate, as he had said. I wanted it more than I'd ever wanted anything in my life. This was *right*—I felt it in my soul. So the only question was, could I achieve it?

"I want to try taking both at once," I told Tark. "But...I've never had anything in my, uh, rosebud. So I'm just not sure how it would work."

"Well, first I need to loosen you up." As he spoke, he reached under me and slid one long finger into the mouth of my pussy. I moaned softly and watched as he gathered some of the cream he'd spurted in me earlier and then slipped lower to massage it into my tight rosebud.

"Oh!" I moaned, wiggling against his invading finger. "Oh, Tark—that feels so…it feels *naughty*. Maybe even *dirty.*"

"I just gave you a nice long bath, Babygirl," he reminded me. "You're not dirty and your sweet little rosebud will be able to open for me once I massage my cream in."

As he spoke, I felt his thick finger sliding inside me but to my surprise, there was no pain—just a stretchy sensation that sent shivers of pure sensation down my spine.

"Mmm…" I moaned softly wiggling on his lap. "That actually feels *good!*"

"That's because you're being a good girl and opening for my fingers," he growled softly. He withdrew for a moment but only to add a second finger. Gently, he scissored them inside me as I gasped and shifted my hips, trying to get used to being touched in such a sensitive, intimate area.

At last Tark seemed to think I was open enough because he withdrew his fingers and gave me a serious look.

"All right, now that your pussy and ass are both nice and open, it's time. Are you ready, Babygirl? Ready to let me double-fuck you and bind you to me?"

"Yes!" I told him. "I want you in me, Tark. I want to feel you deep inside my pussy and ass."

My dirty words seemed to do something to him because his eyes blazed like melted gold and a low growl of pure lust came from his throat.

"Gods, Babygirl! You don't know what it does to me to hear you say that! All right then—get up on your hands and knees in the breeding position."

"Breeding position?" I asked, looking at him with wide eyes.

"That's right, Babygirl. I'm going to be breeding you tonight," he told me. "And I have to warn you—there's a good chance you'll get pregnant from being double fucked."

"I don't mind," I said bravely. "I just want you in me."

"Good girl," he rumbled. "Then get on your hands and knees for me and spread your legs nice and wide."

Feeling nervous but also so turned on I could barely breathe, I climbed off his lap and did as he said. Turning to face away from the big Orc, I got on my hands and knees and spread my thighs. I even arched my back to give him a better view of my pussy and ass. I had never felt so naked or so vulnerable with my bare breasts hanging down, my nipples tight with anticipation.

Tark sucked in a breath.

"Gods, you don't know what it does to me to see you in breeding position, Babygirl," he growled. "I'm going to breed you long and hard tonight. Are you ready for that?"

"Yes," I panted breathlessly. "I'm ready. Fill me up with both your shafts!"

"That's exactly what I'm going to do, Babygirl," he promised me. And then he was kneeling behind me and rubbing the broad head of his larger shaft against my sensitive, swollen clit.

I was quivering with fear and anticipation—could I really take this massive thing inside me? But I trusted Tark not to hurt me and sure enough, he eased in gently and slowly.

"Oh, Tark!" I moaned as I felt the broad head breach my entrance. "Oh, I can feel you going inside of me!"

"That's right, and your sweet little pussy is stretching open to take my thick cock," he growled. "Gods, look at you take it! You're being such a good girl for me, Babygirl. I'm so proud of you!"

"Put more of it inside me!" I demanded breathlessly. "I want you deeper inside me—want to feel you stretching my pussy with your thick cock!"

"That's exactly what I'm going to do," he growled. And then I felt the massive shaft sliding deeper inside me.

I don't know what kind of magic was in the cream his smaller shaft produced, but it really did help me open. I could feel my inner walls being stretched to the limit, but somehow it didn't hurt. Well, not much—there *was* a slight, stretching kind of pain but it felt good too, if that makes any sense. I also loved the feeling of his pleasure ridges entering me. They gave me intense pleasure as they rubbed against my inner channel.

And then, just as he was about halfway inside me, I felt something else. It was the head of his smaller shaft pressing directly against my rosebud.

"Oh, Tark!" I moaned, wiggling my hips. I was already half impaled on his thick lower shaft and I didn't see how my body could take anymore. "I...I feel you back there," I told him.

"That's right, baby—that's my other shaft," he told me. "Just try to relax and be open so I can slip it in your tight little rosebud."

As he spoke, he gripped my hips tightly and I felt him thrusting forward with both shafts. Soon the smaller shaft was sliding into my back entrance even as the bigger one was filling up my pussy.

"Tark!" I gasped, arching my back and gripping the red fur coverlet tight in both fists. "Oh God, you feel so big inside me! Love to feel you filling me up!"

"Gods, Babygirl—can't believe you're taking me so well," he rumbled. "I wish you could see how your sweet little ass and pussy are stretching to take both of my shafts."

"Deeper!" I demanded, wiggling my hips. "I want to feel you all the way inside me."

"That's exactly what I want too, baby," he assured me. And then, with a final thrust, I felt the broad head of his lower shaft meet the end of my channel. At the same time, his muscular hips came flush with my ass, which was filled with his upper shaft and I knew he was all the way in.

"Gods, you're tight!" he groaned. "Never knew humans had such tight pussies!"

"I...I never knew Orcs had...had two cocks," I panted out, wiggling my hips to get used to having him so deep inside me. God, it felt so good to be so full! I had never felt so opened...so owned. And I loved it! "Fill me up, Tark!" I moaned. "Fuck me nice and deep—I want you to! *Breed me!*"

"That's exactly what I'm going to do, Babygirl," he growled.

"Gonna breed you hard tonight!"

Then he gripped my hips even harder and pulled back so that he was halfway out of me. With a low groan, he shoved in again and I gasped as his pleasure ridges rubbed against my G-spot.

Being fucked—especially double-fucked—by a full-blooded Orc is no joke. I couldn't even stay all the way upright. After the first few hard thrusts, I was driven from my hands and knees to my hands and elbows. And after that, all I could do was hang my head, grip the fur coverlet, and hold on for dear life as I spread my thighs as wide as I could, trying to be open enough to take him.

"Oh...oh, Tark!" I heard myself moaning as he fucked me and my breasts swayed with each deep thrust. "Oh God, yes—deeper! More!"

"Look at you being such a good girl," he growled in my ear. "Being so nice and open for my cocks. That's right—keep your soft little pussy and ass spread wide for me so I can fill you with my cream. Might even plant a baby in your belly tonight."

"Yes, Tark," I moaned softly. "Fuck me and fill me up! You can plant a baby in me if you want to—I just want to feel you inside me!"

"Good girl," he groaned again. "Then get ready because I'm going to come in you soon. Do you think you can be sweet and come for me at the same time so I can feel you?"

As he spoke, he slipped one big hand under me and I felt his long fingers parting my pussy lips. I moaned and jerked my hips as he began to slide the pad of one finger around and around my swollen clit, sending me right to the edge of orgasm almost at once.

"Oh, Tark!" I moaned as I bucked against him. "Oh God, yes—I can come for you. Just keep touching me—keep fucking me!"

"Not gonna stop until I feel you coming all over my cocks, Babygirl," he growled. "Want to feel you squeezing me with your tight little pussy and ass!"

As he spoke, I suddenly felt my pussy start to spasm around his thickness. God, I was coming—coming harder than I ever had in my life!

"Oh…*Ohhhh!*" I gasped, bucking my hips helplessly as the pleasure rushed over me in waves. I could feel my inner walls contracting, squeezing his thick cock—almost milking it, as though I was begging him to fill me with his cream.

I knew Tark could feel it too because he suddenly thrust deep inside me and held still with his hands gripped tight around my hips.

"Gods, Babygirl, I can feel you coming all around me!" he groaned. "Your sweet little pussy and ass are milking me! It's like you're *begging* me to breed you!"

"I am!" I moaned. "Oh God, Tark—please come in me! Please make me yours!"

I didn't have to ask him again. Before I knew it, something hot and wet was spurting deep inside me, making me moan even more.

The sensation of him filling me with his cream—with his seed—was almost more than I could stand. I don't know if there was more magic involved, but I do know the feeling of an even deeper and more intense orgasm shot through my whole body and made me moan his name.

"Tark…*Tark!*"

I don't know how long the orgasm lasted, but I felt something happening as I came. It was almost like something was growing between me and Tark. Something that had been planted earlier—maybe even the first time we met. Something that had been strengthened when he first tasted me and made me come and was now fully grown. It seemed to twine around me like an invisible golden vine and I felt it twining around Tark at the same time.

"Gods, Babygirl—I can feel us coming together," he groaned. "You're mine now—you'll always be mine! And I'll always be yours."

"Always!" I moaned. "Oh God, Tark—*always.*"

I knew that we would never be apart now that I was…*Loved by the Orc.*

20

HARMONY

After he finally pulled out of me, Tark had to give me another bath, to clean me up. But it wasn't until we came back in the bedroom to strip the sheets, that we got a surprise.

"Hey—why is this so heavy?" he grumbled, when he took hold of the headboard to shift it a little to one side. "It's never felt like this before."

"I don't know—I was hanging on to it while you, er, tasted me," I said. I was wrapped in another one of his big, puffy towels that was more like a blanket. If you've never tried Orc sized towels, I highly recommend them.

"Ah...I thought I felt something happening when you were coming." He nodded wisely.

"What? What happened? What are you talking about?" I demanded.

"I mean, this..." He wrapped one big hand around the top rail of the brass headboard and I saw his bicep bulge as he lifted it. When he let it drop, it came down with a dull *thunk!* that shook the floor!

"Oh!" I exclaimed. "What happened to it to make it so heavy?"

"You did, Babygirl." He rumbled laughter, his eyes dancing. "You turned it to gold when you came!"

"I *did?*" I went to put a hand on the brass headboard. Maybe it was a little different color than it had been before, I thought. But nothing extraordinary. Tark was right, though—it was too heavy for me to even *try* lifting it.

"Solid gold," he confirmed, still chuckling. "Well, I guess now we know your magic works either when you're in mortal peril or when you're coming."

"Wow…" I shook my head. "Well, I know which one I'd rather be doing."

"You can make millions and billions, you know—if you want to." Tark's eyes were suddenly serious. "You can turn yourself into a dragon and live in a castle—a literal one—if you want."

"But what if I'd rather just stay here with you and learn from Madam Healer?" I asked, looking up at him.

He came around the bed and took me in his arms.

"That's what I want too, baby. And now that we're Sworn Heartmates, we're going to be together forever. I was just saying, if you wanted to, we could move to the Human Realm and buy a place in one of those ultra fancy high rises or something. It wouldn't be my first choice, but I'll follow wherever you want to go."

"No overpriced penthouse suite could compare with Hidden Hollow," I told him, snuggling to get closer. "I like it here. And now that Mr. Price—or the monster impersonating him—is dead, I think I'm going to have to move here. Like I said, the police would want to question me and what could I say? 'Sorry, my Orc boyfriend chopped off his head because he made me upset so he could suck out my emotions?' I don't think that would go over very well."

Tark rumbled a laugh.

"Yeah, that might be fucking hard to sell. But what about your dream of becoming a pharmacist?"

"I'd rather be an alchemist," I said, lifting my chin. "It's way more interesting and fun." I nibbled my lip. "If…I can live here with you?"

"Of course you can!" Tark exclaimed. "I wanted to ask you to move in earlier, but I was afraid I might scare you off."

"You did?" I raised my eyebrows. "Like how much earlier?"

"Oh, I don't know…pretty much from the first time I saw you when you came running out of that door and smacked right into me." He grinned. "I just knew the minute I saw you that you were for me. Does that sound weird?"

"Not weird at all," I assured him, snuggling against his broad chest. "Oh, Tark—I love you so much!"

"Love you too, Babygirl," he growled softly, stroking my hair. "And now I never have to let you go."

THE END?
CERTAINLY NOT!

I have a lot more ideas for Hidden Hollow coming your way. And I swear at some point I'm going to write Goldie's book. It's just that my pesky Muse keeps giving me other ideas first. But look for Goldie's book, *Warded by the Werebears,* soon as well as another book from Hidden Hollow called *Craved by the Kraken.* I already have the book covers so they could come out anytime my Muse behaves.

As always, if you've enjoyed this book, please take a minute to leave a review. The book market is currently being flooded by AI written books, which is making it harder and harder for 100% human-written books like mine to gain traction. Please support human-only books, audiobooks, and book covers. Otherwise the human artists and creatives working to bring you entertainment will be forced out of this industry. Once that happens, true creativity will be gone for good and everything you read, watch, and listen to will start sounding the same. I don't want that and I'm sure you don't either. So please be mindful and try to buy human written books.

Hugs and thanks for being an awesome reader!
Evangeline (Feb 2025)

PS—next is the Bonus Daddy Section for those of you who have a Daddy Kink. Enjoy! ;)

BONUS DADDY SECTION

These are basically the same chapters that appear in the main book, except there has been some sweet and spicy Daddy content added. If you do not have a Daddy Kink, please ignore this section and go back to the regular book.

8. HARMONY
(BONUS SECTION)

Tark cuddled me close, stroking my hair.

"You know, in some Orc Tribes they have a custom—a kind of relationship between a male and a female when she's been orphaned," he murmured.

"What kind of relationship?" I asked, snuggling closer to him. It seemed like I just couldn't get close enough.

"It might sound kind of strange to you," Tark said. "But the male sometimes acts like a kind of father figure to the female who's been orphaned. I need to point out that it only happens among consenting adults—those who have come of age," he added quickly.

"So...how is that different from what you're doing right now?" I asked, looking up at him.

"Well, he doesn't just comfort her—he *cares* for her," Tark said carefully. "Like...he bathes her and chooses her clothes and dresses and undresses her and cooks for her. He lets her just be *little,* if that makes sense. It allows her to regain some of the childhood that she lost—to feel the love she missed when her parents passed into the Beyond."

"I *think* I know what you're talking about," I said slowly. "I've read about something like that in the, uh, 'Human Realm.' It's some kind of a kink."

"A kink?" He frowned. "What's that?"

"You know—a sexual fetish," I explained, my cheeks getting red. "Like in the human version the girl gets off on calling the guy 'Daddy' sometimes."

Tark gave me a half-lidded look.

"Hmm, I think I like that. But how do *you* feel about it? Would you like to call me 'Daddy?'"

I felt an immediate rush of sensation that ran through my whole body. I wasn't sure why this idea appealed to me so strongly but it did—it *really* did. All my life I'd been missing that sense of caring—that feeling of being protected and loved by a strong male father-figure.

"God, *yes,*" I blurted. "If…if you don't think it's weird. I mean, treating me like I'm little and you're my—"

"Your *protector*—that's what a Daddy is," he said firmly. Stroking my cheek, he looked into my eyes. "And a good Daddy will always take care of his Babygirl. You know that, right?"

My breath seemed to catch in my throat.

"Take care of me *how*, Daddy?" I asked softly, rubbing against him.

"Mmm, how would you *like* me to take care of you, baby?" he rumbled, his eyes lazy with lust.

Being that close to him when I was feeling so many emotions—feeling so open and vulnerable with him—seemed to be doing something to my body. Pressing my face to his neck, I breathed him in and felt myself reacting to his wild, woodsy scent. My nipples were suddenly hard and between my thighs I felt wet and ready.

"How do you think?" I whispered. I rubbed against him, moaning softly as my tight nipples pressed against his broad chest. God, what was wrong with me? One minute I was bawling my eyes out and the next I was so horny I felt like I might crawl out of my skin!

Tark sensed the shift in me because when he pulled back from our embrace to look at me, his golden eyes were half-lidded.

"Mmm, what's going on with you, Babygirl?" he murmured. "Feeling some kind of way, are you? Like you need Daddy to take care of you?"

"I *might* be," I admitted breathlessly. "Tark…I think…no, I *know*—I want to be naked with you. And…and let you take care of me."

His eyes blazed and then went lazy with lust and his voice dropped to a soft growl.

"I don't know if you're ready for that yet, baby."

"Yes, I am," I insisted. "I know we haven't been together that long but I trust you! And I want…no, I *need* to be close to you. With no clothes on."

"All right, but we're taking it slow," he said. "And we're not going further than I think you can handle."

Then he lifted me in his arms and carried me into the bedroom.

9. HARMONY
(BONUS SECTION)

Tark lay me down gently on his enormous bed and I felt like a princess in a fairytale. He had a deep red coverlet that was made of some kind of extremely soft fur. It felt amazing against my cheek when I rubbed against it—I wondered how it would feel against my nude body.

I'll admit, I was a little shy to be naked in front of him—especially after hearing how "fat" I was from Mr. Price. But the curtains were drawn and the day outside was cloudy, which meant the bedroom was quite dim. So when Turk took off his shirt and then got on the bed with me, I started unbuttoning my blouse.

"No, wait—let me," he rumbled, putting one big hand on mine to stop me.

I looked up at him.

"You want to…"

"I want to undress you. Didn't I say I was going to take care of you, baby?" he asked.

"Yes." I nodded.

"Good, then let me do this."

He began unbuttoning the little pearl buttons on my blouse and as he did, he leaned forward and began laying hot, gentle kisses on my bare throat.

"*Ohhh*," I moaned as his hot, wet mouth traveled up and down my neck and then down to my chest, just above my breasts.

"Mmm, Babygirl, your skin tastes so sweet," he murmured as he slipped the blouse all the way off. "Are you ready to let Daddy take off your bra now?"

"Yes, Daddy." I nodded. My breasts were actually a part of me I liked and Tark seemed to like them too.

"Gods, look at those sweet nipples," he growled softly as he helped me out of my bra. He cupped my right breast in his left hand and gently thumbed the nipple, making me squirm. "You like that, Babygirl? You want Daddy to suck your sweet nipples for you?"

"Y-yes," I whispered breathlessly.

"Then ask me—ask me to do it," he urged, his voice rough with desire.

"Please, Daddy—I want you to suck my nipples," I moaned, thrusting my breast further into his hand.

"Good girl—love to hear you ask me for what you want—what you *need*," he murmured. Then he bent his head over my chest and swirled his tongue lightly around my left nipple. At the same time, he was still tugging and teasing my right nipple with his fingers.

I gasped and arched my back—it felt so *good*. And I loved the way he was teasing me. His hot mouth on my sensitive peaks was driving me *crazy*.

Tark took his time, going back and forth and sucking each nipple in turn. Sometimes he teased me with his tongue and then he would suck my tight peak deep and hard, sending sparks of pleasure/pain from my sensitive tips straight to my pussy. I was getting so hot and wet by now that I didn't know how much more I could take.

"Please, Daddy!" I begged breathlessly. "Please, I need *more*."

He sucked my nipple even harder for a moment, making me gasp, before finally looking up.

"Mmm, babygirl—what's wrong? Are you feeling all achy between your legs?" he rumbled.

Biting my lip, I nodded.

"Yes, I am. I want…I want more of you. And I want you to have more of me!"

Tark gave me a stern look.

"Tell me what you mean, baby—tell me what you want."

"I want…" I bit my lip and pressed my thighs together. "I want you to touch me, Daddy," I confessed at last.

"Like this, you mean?" And he slid one big hand into the waistband of my skirt and cupped my pussy through my lace panties.

"*Ohhh*," I moaned softly and rubbed shamelessly against his fingers. "Yes, like that! Only even *more.*"

"Hmm, Babygirl—are you asking Daddy to pet your soft little pussy without your panties on?"

I could feel my cheeks heating with a blush but the intent way he was looking at me made me feel like I *had* to answer.

"Yes, Daddy," I said in a small voice. "I want…I *need* you to pet my bare pussy."

"Mmm, I'd be happy to do that for you, Babygirl. Daddy loves to pet his baby's pussy," he growled. "But first let's get this off."

He removed my skirt, sliding it slowly down my legs. Now all I was wearing was my white lace panties. I felt a shiver of vulnerability go through me, but the way Tark was looking at me made me feel beautiful.

"Gods, baby—so fucking gorgeous," he growled hoarsely, looking me up and down. "Love your sweet little body! Come here."

And pulling me close, he fit me into the crook of his arm so that he was lying on his side and I was on my back with my head pillowed on one broad bicep.

"Now look at me while I touch you," he ordered, slipping his fingers beneath the waistband of my panties. "Look at Daddy while he pets your soft little pussy."

As he spoke, I felt his long fingers parting the outer lips of my pussy. I gasped and jerked my hips as they slipped into my wet interior and found the aching button of my clit.

"Oh, did Daddy find a sensitive spot?" Tark raised an eyebrow at me, grinning a little. "Does it feel good when I touch you there?"

"Yes, Daddy!" I moaned as he began to circle my clit gently with one fingertip. "It feels…feels really *good*."

"That's because you're being a good girl and spreading your sweet pussy for Daddy," he growled softly. "Does it feel good when Daddy pets you here?"

"It feels *so* good, Daddy!" I moaned. "I…I think I might come soon."

His eyes went half-lidded and a deep growl that was pure lust came from his throat.

"Gods, Babygirl—Daddy wants to make you come! But not like this."

And to my dismay, he pulled his long fingers out of my panties.

"Daddy!" I nearly wailed. "What are you doing? I was so *close*."

"But you need to get even closer, Babygirl. Don't worry, I'm going to make you come. But not with my fingers."

And then he sat up, hooked his thumbs in the waistband of my panties, and pulled them all the way off.

"Oh, Tark!" I exclaimed. I felt suddenly shy, being completely nude like this. The red fur coverlet was incredibly soft against my bare skin as I rolled over to cover myself with my arms.

"No, baby…" Tark shook his head as he pushed me gently but firmly back onto my back. Then he put his hands on my knees and began pulling my legs apart.

"Oh! What are you doing?" I asked, biting my lip.

"Daddy needs you to open for him now, Babygirl," he said sternly.

I nibbled my lip some more.

"Why, Daddy?" I asked softly.

"So Daddy can taste you," he rumbled, his eyes blazing.

I felt an immediate surge of self-doubt. I'd never had a guy go down on me before.

"What…what if you don't like it, though?" I asked softly. "Like, what if you don't like the taste or the smell or…"

Tark silenced me by putting the two fingers he'd been using to stroke me earlier into his mouth. He sucked them, his golden eyes half-lidded as he looked at me. My heart was racing as he finally cleaned all my juices off his fingers and pulled them out of his mouth.

"Spread for me, Babygirl," he growled and it wasn't a request. "Let Daddy eat that sweet little pussy."

Feeling like my heart might beat its way right out of my chest, I did as he ordered.

"Good girl. Goddess—look how wet you are!" he murmured as he got into position between my thighs. He was so big that his broad shoulders split me wide, making my pussy open even more for him.

I felt a rush of embarrassment laced with desire as he looked down at me. His face said he was looking at a rare treasure—one he'd been longing to own.

"Been wanting to do this from the first minute you ran into me out in the middle of Main Street," he growled, looking up at me. "Now spread nice and wide for Daddy so he can taste his babygirl's pussy."

"Yes, Daddy," I murmured submissively. Seeing how much he wanted to do this definitely put me more at ease. I was still a little nervous about being so spread out for him, but not as uncertain as I had been before he reassured me.

"Mmm, Babygirl…" he rumbled. Leaning forward, he rubbed one bristly cheek against the soft curls on my mound, making me moan and buck my hips.

Tark looked up at me, his eyes filled with lust.

"Sorry, Babygirl—was that too scratchy for you? Is your soft little pussy sensitive?"

"Yes, I…I think it is," I admitted breathlessly.

"I promise to be more gentle, then," he growled softly. "Like this…"

And leaning over again, he placed a hot, open mouthed kiss directly on my open pussy.

I moaned and wiggled my hips as his tongue slid deep, caressing my clit as he kissed my pussy the same way he kissed my mouth.

"Oh, Daddy!" I moaned and slid my hands into his hair. He was so big and strong he could have broken me in half without even trying but instead he was being so sweet to me—so gentle, just like he'd promised and I loved it!

I slid my fingers into his coarse black hair because I had to have something to hold on to as he continued to explore me with his tongue. He was flicking my clit with the tip of his tongue and then I felt two long, thick fingers sliding inside me.

"Oh! Oh, Tark! Daddy!" I gasped, arching my back and bucking my hips as his fingers filled me to the hilt. "Oh God, yes—just like that!"

Tark growled deep in his throat and redoubled his efforts. Sucking my clit into his mouth he began to tease and lick it over and over while at the same time he was fucking me with those thick fingers.

And then I felt something different—he wasn't just thrusting into me anymore, he was rubbing—rubbing the inner walls of my pussy. It felt like he had found another clit, there inside me. But the feelings he was giving me were even deeper and more primal and they were pushing me closer and closer to the edge of coming.

"Oh!" I moaned as the pleasure overtook me. "Oh, *Daddy!* Tark— yes! Oh, God, *yes!*"

I don't know what I was babbling, but I was pulling his hair and bucking my hips like a madwoman. I couldn't help myself—no one but me had ever made me come before and the feeling of being completely out of control while the pleasure soared through me was almost too much!

As the intense sensations went on and on, I felt something else inside me—something powerful uncurling—something that had perhaps lay dormant or sleeping all of my life, felt like it was waking up. But what was it?

I didn't know and I couldn't analyze it—not when I was coming so hard. I didn't know how he was doing it but Tark seemed to be drawing out my orgasm, making it last somehow. My toes curled and my back arched…then I started seeing black spots dancing in front of my eyes.

"Oh!" I gasped. "Oh God, Tark…I can't…I think I'm going to…going to…"

But before I could get the words "I'm going to faint" out of my mouth, everything went black.

Author's Note — *From here you can return to Chapter 10 (Page 70) in the main book to continue the story. There will be more "Daddy Chapters" later on in the book but I will have a note by them so you know when to come back to the Bonus Daddy section. ;) Evangeline*

17. HARMONY
(BONUS SECTION)

As soon as we got back to his house, Tark insisted on running me a bath in his enormous bathtub.

"I'm honestly all right. I don't need a bath," I protested as I sank in up to my neck. "Ooo—ouch!" I added, because my cuts were stinging.

"You were saying?" Tark raised one sardonic eyebrow at me as he wetted a sponge and began to gently scrub me.

"Hey, it's just because the hot water stings," I said defensively.

"Exactly—it stings because you were scratched by a demon—a Sin Sucker," he said firmly. "We have to get those cuts *completely* clean before I put the healing salve on."

"Why?" I asked nervously. "Will they make me sick? Give me blood poisoning?"

"Worse—they could give you *soul* poisoning if we're not careful," he said grimly. "And you don't want that—the evil that was in the monster that attacked you could reach your heart and turn it as hard and cold as his was."

"No, I definitely don't want that!" I shivered. The thought of becoming like Mr. Price chilled me, even though I was neck deep in hot, soapy water.

"Of course you don't. Don't worry, baby—we're going to get you squeaky clean tonight," he promised. "Just let Daddy wash you."

Hearing him say that gave me a warm safe feeling and I sank down in the tub and let him do what he wanted with me. After all, I was his Babygirl—I liked it when he took control.

He took his time, scrubbing me all over—and I do mean *all* over. He ran his big hands all over my body until I was practically trembling with need. But though he took the time to tug my nipples and to scrub between my legs—which mostly consisted of him teasing my aching clit with his fingertip—he never quite let me come.

At last I was panting with need.

"Please, Daddy!" I begged. "Please, I need you!"

"Need you too, baby," he growled softly. "You think you're all clean now? Or should Daddy wash your soft little pussy some more?"

"All clean and ready for naked cuddles," I assured him. "And this time I want you to get naked too!"

Tark gave me an uncertain look.

"I still don't know if you're ready for that, Babygirl. Remember I told you that Orcs have different, uh, equipment down there?"

"What, do you have a nest of tentacles or something?" I demanded, feeling thoroughly exasperated.

He rumbled a laugh.

"Hardly! I'm not a fucking Kraken, you know."

"Well, whatever you have, I want to see it," I said bossily. "And more than that, I want to *use* it. I nearly died today, you know. And if I had, I would have gone without ever getting to get really close to you."

"Aw, Babygirl—please don't talk like that!" His golden eyes were suddenly suspiciously shiny.

"Well, it's true," I pointed out. I sighed. "Look, I know you think I'm too small to, you know, take you, but at least let me *try*. I have some pretty big toys back home, you know."

His eyes were suddenly lazy with lust.

"Toys, is it? Hmm, why is this the first I'm hearing about them?"

I bit my lip, my cheeks feeling hot.

"Well…I mean, it's kind of embarrassing. But I wanted you to know that I can take you."

"You'll probably be able to if I taste you first," he rumbled. "The question is, will you want to once you see what I've got in my pants?"

"What in the *world* do you have?" I demanded—I was extremely curious. "Come on, you *have* to show me."

Tark sighed.

"Well… I guess. But it's different from what human males have."

"Tark…" I put my hand on his arm and looked into his eyes. "Whatever it is, I want it," I told him. "You love and accept me just the way I am—what makes you think I can't do the same for you?"

"I just don't want to scare you off," he said in a low voice. "You mean a lot to me, Babygirl—I've never felt this way for any woman before."

I felt like my heart was swelling with his words.

"I've never felt like this for anyone before, either," I said softly. "And you won't scare me off—I'm not going anywhere."

"All right, Babygirl—you asked for it." He had been kneeling by the tub but now he rose and held open a fluffy blue towel for me. "Come on—let's get you all dried off and then you can see what Daddy has for you."

18. HARMONY
(BONUS SECTION)

Tark finished drying me off and then swung me into his arms and carried me into the bedroom. The minute he put me down in the center of his huge bed, I was reaching for him.

"Come here, Daddy—cuddle me!" I demanded. "But first take off your jeans!"

He did as I asked, but I noticed that he left his underwear—which were black boxer-briefs—on. I started to protest, but he shook his head.

"No, baby—let me at least get you ready first. Then you can decide if you like what you see of not."

"Get me ready? How?" I asked frowning as he climbed on the bed with me.

"Like this," he growled. And reaching for me, he wrapped his massive hands around my waist and lifted me.

"Oh, Daddy! What…what are you doing?" I gasped, but I had my answer soon enough. He was lying flat on his back and positioning himself so that I was straddling his head.

"There," he growled, looked up at me with half-lidded eyes. "Now we're ready."

"Ready for what?" I squeaked.

"Ready for Daddy to taste you, Babygirl." And tugging on my hips, he pulled me lower until my pussy was positioned right over his mouth.

"Oh…oh, Daddy!" I gasped. "Don't—I'll smother you!"

He gave a hungry laugh.

"Then fucking *smother* me, baby! I can't think of a better way to go." His eyes roved over my body and went half-lidded. "Goddess, look at that soft little pussy, just begging to be tasted by Daddy! Can't wait to feel my Babygirl coming on my tongue."

"I mean it," I protested, still resisting as he tugged on my hips. "I'll *crush* you!"

He barked another laugh.

"Have you seen how big I am, baby? There's no way you can crush me with your soft, curvy little body. Now come on—if you want a look at what I have down below, I need to taste you first. Just in case one thing leads to another. Are you going to be a good girl and let Daddy eat your sweet pussy?"

I still wasn't quite sure, but I finally allowed him to tug me down until my pussy was in contact with his mouth.

I heard a low growl of approval and then I moaned in surprised pleasure as his warm, wet tongue invaded me. Leaning forward, I gripped the top of the headboard, trying to keep my balance as he began licking me in earnest.

"Oh…*ohhh!*" I heard myself moaning as I felt his tongue sliding deep inside me and then swiping up to tease my aching clit. "Oh, Daddy—that feels so *good!*"

At first I tried to grip the top of the brass headboard and keep myself from putting too much pressure on his face, but Tark wasn't having that.

"Come here, baby—let Daddy taste you!"

With a low, possessive growl, he gripped my hips even tighter and brought me down, insisting that I sit fully on his face without holding back.

I probably would have killed a human man that way, but a full—

blooded Orc is a whole different kind of male. Tark seemed to be having no difficulty at all handling my weight—in fact, he seemed to *love* it. He was making low, hungry growling sounds as he ate me and I began to feel more free when I realized how much he was enjoying himself.

Gripping the top railing of the brass headboard harder, I began to ride him—pressing my pussy fully against his mouth. Somehow he managed to keep from cutting me with his tusks, though I could feel them bracketing my pussy as I rubbed against him.

"Daddy!" I moaned as I rode his face. "Oh God, that feels so good! Love to have your tongue in my pussy! Love to feel you tasting me!"

I had never been so vocal during sex before but it felt good to let loose and I could tell that Tark liked it too. He growled approvingly and licked me even harder as I ground myself against his mouth shamelessly.

My pleasure was already building and I began to get nervous when I realized how close I was to coming. Was I going to faint again? I thought I could feel a slight tingling in my fingertips but when I looked at them, I couldn't tell if they were glowing or not.

I would have stopped the big Orc if I could have, but by that time Tark was completely unstoppable. His long fingers were curled around my waist and his tongue was lashing me, teasing my swollen clit until I couldn't help myself anymore.

"Oh....oh, Daddy!" I moaned as my orgasm rolled over me in a wave of sensation.

And then I was coming—coming so hard I was seeing stars flashing in front of my eyes. I gasped and rubbed myself against his wet tongue even harder as I gripped the headboard tighter. Oh God, it felt so good…so *fucking good!*

I squeezed my eyes shut and felt power running through my body as I went rigid with pleasure, my toes curling and my back arching. What was happening? What was I doing?

But when I finally opened my eyes, feeling apprehensive to see what my magic might have done, nothing looked different. The shiny brass headboard was still the same as far as I could see and Tark seemed fine—though he showed no signs of stopping.

"Tark…Daddy, please!" I moaned, trying to pull away as his tongue lashed my overly sensitive clit again. "I need a minute before you make me come again!"

He finally heard me because he loosened his grip on my hips and I was able to pull away from his mouth. When I looked down at him, his eyes were blazing and his lips were wet with my juices.

"Gods, Babygirl—fucking love the way your soft little pussy tastes!" he growled. "You're such a good girl to spread your legs for Daddy and let him taste you. I never want to fucking stop!"

"I can tell." I gave a shaky laugh. "But it's my turn now. You promised if I let you, er, taste me, that you'd let me see your equipment."

He sighed.

"Oh, right. Well…okay. But don't blame me if it scares you."

And with those cryptic words, he lifted me away from his face and tucked me into the crook of his arm instead.

19. HARMONY
(BONUS SECTION)

I couldn't help noticing that there was an extremely large tent in the stretchy black material of his boxer-briefs. It drew me like a magnet and I reached for him at once.

"Easy, Babygirl," he rumbled, putting a hand over mine. "I know you're eager for your prize, but let's go slow."

"I'm tired of going slow!" I protested. "Let me see it!"

"All right…you asked for it."

With a sigh, he peeled down the waistband of his boxer-briefs revealing…

"Oh my God," I said blankly. "You've got *two* of them."

"All Orcs do," Tark told me.

I stared in surprise at the two shafts that had been revealed when he pulled down his shorts. One of them—the bottom one—was absolutely massive. It was even bigger than my biggest toy, I thought as apprehension raced through me. Topped with a broad, flaring crown, it had a shaft so thick I didn't think I could even fit my fingers around it, let alone fit it in my pussy! It was also covered with parallel lines—raised ridges that ran the entire length of it on both the top and bottom sides.

The second shaft was situated directly above the larger one. It was considerably smaller, though still a good size. It was also shorter. At least there was only one set of balls, I thought. They were massive and located right under the larger shaft.

It was surprising, I'll admit. But no matter how daunting the situation was, I wasn't giving up! I wanted to make love with Tark—I wanted him inside me.

"Okay, tell me all about this," I said and reached out to take the smaller shaft in my hand. "How does it work? Am I supposed to ride the smaller one first and then try the bigger one?"

"Actually, that's a good idea. Gods, your soft little hands feel good on me!" he groaned. "The top shaft—my secondary shaft—makes a special cum that helps you open for my bottom shaft. It also rubs against your clit and makes it swell and become more sensitive—that way you can come again when I fuck you."

"Mmm, I like that idea," I told him.

"Then climb on board, Babygirl," he growled. "Let me just get settled here…" He propped some pillows against the headboard and then motioned for me. "Come here and let Daddy fuck you."

His dirty words made me feel hot all over again. I straddled his lap eagerly and rubbed the head of the smaller shaft against my open pussy. At once a warming precum started flowing from its tip. As I rubbed it against me, I could feel my clit swelling and getting even more sensitive.

"Oh!" I exclaimed, looking down at myself. My pussy was open and wet and I was aching inside—as though I needed to be filled.

"That's right, Babygirl—Gods, look at how hot and wet your soft little pussy is," Tark growled. "Just lower yourself down on my upper shaft—need to come in you with the top shaft in order to help you open for the bottom one."

Moaning softly, I did as he said. I could feel the second, larger shaft rubbing against my behind as I leaned forward and lowered myself down on the top one.

Even though it was smaller than the bottom shaft, it was still big enough to fill me and stretch my inner walls—which was exactly what I felt like I needed. I wiggled as I felt it slip all the way inside, the head pressing against the end of my channel.

"That's right, Babygirl," Tark growled softly. "Now just wait a minute…Gods!" He stifled a groan and then I felt something hot and wet spurting deep inside me. Was this the special cum that would help me take his larger lower shaft? It must be, I decided.

"Oh, Daddy!" I moaned. "I can feel you coming in me—it feels so good!"

"Feels fucking good to me too, Babygirl," he groaned. "Gods your soft little pussy feels so good around me!"

He filled me completely with his cream until it was leaking out even with his smaller shaft fully inside me. When he finally pulled out, I could feel it gushing everywhere. It even slid down and coated my rosebud, making me tingle all over.

"Oh my God—we made a mess!" I said, looking down.

"That's all right," Tark assured me. "As long as it gets everywhere. Because now you have a choice, Babygirl."

"A choice?" I asked, raising my eyebrows. "What choice?"

"You get to pick how you want me to fuck you," he growled softly. Cupping my cheek he looked into my eyes. "We can just do it this way, with you facing me. My larger shaft goes into your pussy and my smaller shaft keeps rubbing against your clit to make you come."

"I like the idea of that," I purred. Though I had enjoyed having his smaller shaft inside me, I was dying to feel the much larger one stretching me out.

"Or…" He held up a finger. "You can choose the other way—it's what we Orcs call 'double fucking' and we only use it when we want to bind a woman-a Heartmate—to us forever."

"Forever?" I asked, my heart leaping in my chest. "Tark, do you really think—"

"I don't just think—I *know*, Babygirl," he said firmly. He stroked my cheek. "I know I want to be with you always—to be your Daddy forever. You're my Heartmate—the one I was always meant to be with. And I'm sure I'm your Heartmate, too. The question is, do you want to stay together and be Sworn to me for the rest of our lives?"

I didn't hesitate a minute.

"Yes!" Leaning forward, I threw my arms around his neck and nuzzled against him. "Yes, that's exactly what I want! But how do we do it?"

"Well, it might be a little challenging for you since you're so little," he rumbled. "But if you think you can take it, we'll try it."

"Try what?" I asked, pulling back to look at him. "What are we going to be doing? Or I guess I should ask, how are we going to be doing it?"

"You have to take both my shafts at once," he explained. "The larger one in your pussy and the smaller one in your tight little rosebud." He gave me a serious look. "Do you think you can do that for me, baby? Do you think you can take both of Daddy's shafts inside you at once?"

I bit my lip, thinking it over. On one hand, my ass was a sensitive area—though I had a lot of toys, I hadn't used many of them there. And while Tark's smaller shaft was considerably less girthy than the big one, it was still enough that I could really feel it opening my pussy. How would it feel in my ass—especially if I was getting skewered by the other, much more massive cock at the same time?

But on the other hand, I wanted to be Sworn to him as his Heartmate, as he had said. I wanted it more than I'd ever wanted anything in my life. This was *right*—I felt it in my soul. So the only question was, could I achieve it.

"I want to try taking both at once," I told Tark. "But…I've never had anything in my, uh, rosebud. So I'm just not sure how it would work."

"Well, first I need to loosen you up." As he spoke, he reached under me and slid one long finger into the mouth of my pussy. I moaned softly and watched as he gathered some of the cream he'd spurted in me earlier and then slipped lower to massage it into my tight rosebud.

"Oh!" I moaned, wiggling against his invading finger. "Oh, Daddy—that feels so…it feels *naughty*. Maybe even *dirty*."

"I just gave you a nice long bath, Babygirl," he reminded me. "You're not dirty and your sweet little rosebud will be able to open for me once I massage my cream in."

As he spoke, I felt his thick finger sliding inside me but to my surprise, there was no pain—just a stretchy sensation that sent shivers down my spine.

"Mmm…" I moaned softly wiggling on his lap. "That actually feels *good*, Daddy!"

"That's because you're being a good girl and opening for Daddy's fingers," he growled softly. He withdrew for a moment but only to add a second finger. Gently, he scissored them inside me as I gasped and shifted my hips, trying to get used to being touched in such a sensitive, intimate area.

At last Tark seemed to think I was open enough because he withdrew his fingers and gave me a serious look.

"All right, now that your pussy and ass are both nice and open, it's time. Are you ready, Babygirl? Ready to let Daddy double-fuck you and bind you to him?"

"Yes!" I told him. "I want you in me, Daddy. I want to feel you deep inside my pussy and ass."

My dirty words seemed to do something to him because his eyes blazed like melted gold and a low growl of pure lust came from his throat.

"Gods, Babygirl! You don't know what it does to me to hear you say that! All right then—get up on your hands and knees in the breeding position."

"Breeding position?" I asked, looking at him with wide eyes.

"That's right, Babygirl. I'm going to be breeding you tonight," he told me. "And I have to warn you—there's a good chance you'll get pregnant from being double fucked."

"I don't mind," I said bravely. "I just want you in me, Daddy."

"Good girl," he rumbled. "Then get on your hands and knees for me and spread your legs nice and wide. Daddy's going to breed you."

Feeling nervous but also so turned on I could barely breathe, I climbed off his lap and did as he said. Turning to face away from the big Orc, I got on my hands and knees and spread my thighs. I even arched my back to give him a better view of my pussy and ass. I had never felt so naked or so vulnerable with my bare breasts hanging down, my nipples tight with anticipation.

Tark sucked in a breath.

"Gods, you don't know what it does to me to see you in breeding position, Babygirl," he growled. "Daddy's going to breed his little girl long and hard tonight. Are you ready for that?"

"Yes, Daddy!" I panted breathlessly. "I'm ready. Fill me up with both your shafts!"

"That's exactly what I'm going to do, Babygirl," he promised me. And then he was kneeling behind me and rubbing the broad head of his larger shaft against my sensitive, swollen clit.

I was quivering with fear and anticipation—could I really take this massive thing inside me? But I trusted Tark not to hurt me and sure enough, he eased in gently and slowly.

"Oh, Daddy!" I moaned as I felt the broad head breach my entrance. "Oh, I can feel you going inside of me!"

"That's right, and your sweet little pussy is stretching open to take Daddy's thick cock," he growled. "Gods, look at you take it! You're being such a good girl for Daddy, Babygirl. I'm so proud of you!"

"Put more of it inside me!" I demanded breathlessly. "I want you deeper inside me, Daddy—want to feel you stretching my pussy with your thick cock!"

"That's exactly what I'm going to do," he growled. And then I felt the massive shaft sliding deeper inside me.

I don't know what kind of magic was in the cream his smaller shaft produced, but it really did help me open. I could feel my inner walls being stretched to the limit, but somehow it didn't hurt. Well, not much—there *was* a slight, stretching kind of pain but it felt good too, if that makes any sense. I also loved the feeling of his pleasure ridges entering me. They gave me intense pleasure as they rubbed against my inner channel.

And then, just as he was about halfway inside me, I felt something else. It was the head of his smaller shaft pressing directly against my rosebud.

"Oh, Daddy!" I moaned, wiggling my hips. I was already half impaled on his thick lower shaft and I didn't see how my body could take anymore. "I…I feel you back there," I told him.

"That's right, baby—that's Daddy's other shaft," he told me. "Just try to relax and be open so I can slip it in your tight little rosebud."

As he spoke, he gripped my hips tightly and I felt him thrusting forward with both shafts. Soon the smaller shaft was sliding into my tight rosebud even as the bigger one was filling up my pussy.

"Daddy!" I gasped, arching my back and gripping the red fur coverlet tight in both fists. "Oh God, you feel so big inside me! Love to feel you filling me up!"

"Gods, Babygirl—can't believe you're taking me so well," he rumbled. "I wish you could see how your sweet little ass and pussy are stretching to take both of Daddy's shafts."

"Deeper!" I demanded, wiggling my hips. "I want to feel you all the way inside me."

"That's exactly what I want too, baby," he assured me. And then, with a final thrust, I felt the broad head of his lower shaft meet the end of my channel. At the same time, his muscular hips came flush with my ass, which was filled with his upper shaft and I knew he was all the way in.

"Gods, you're tight!" he groaned. "Never knew humans had such tight pussies!"

"I...I never knew Orcs had...had two cocks," I panted out, wiggling my hips to get used to having him so deep inside me. God, it felt so good to be so full! I had never felt so opened...so owned. And I loved it! "Fill me up, Daddy!" I moaned. "Fuck me nice and deep—I want you to!"

"That's exactly what I want too, Babygirl," he growled. Then he gripped my hips even harder and pulled back so that he was halfway out of me. With a low groan, he shoved in again and I gasped as his pleasure ridges rubbed against my G-spot.

Being fucked—especially double-fucked—by a full-blooded Orc is no joke. I couldn't even stay all the way upright. After the first few hard thrusts, I was driven from my hands and knees to my hands and elbows. And after that, all I could do was hang my head and hold on for dear life as I spread my thighs as wide as I could, trying to be open enough to take him.

"Oh...oh, Daddy!" I heard myself moaning as he fucked me. "Oh God, yes—deeper! More!"

"Look at you being such a good girl," he growled in my ear. "Being so nice and open for Daddy's cocks. That's right—keep your soft little pussy and ass spread for Daddy so I can fill you with my cream. Might even plant a baby in your belly tonight."

"Yes, Daddy," I moaned softly. "Fuck me and fill me up! You can plant a baby in me if you want to—I just want to feel you inside me!"

"Good girl," he groaned again. "Then get ready because Daddy's going to come in you soon. Do you think you can be sweet and come for me at the same time so I can feel you?"

As he spoke, he slipped one big hand under me and I felt his long fingers parting my pussy lips. I moaned and jerked my hips as he began to slide the pad of one finger around and around my swollen clit, sending me right to the edge of orgasm almost at once.

"Oh, Daddy!" I moaned as I bucked against him. "Oh God, yes—I can come for you. Just keep touching me—keep fucking me!"

"Not gonna stop until I feel you coming all over my cocks,

Babygirl," he growled. "Want to feel you squeezing me with your tight little pussy and ass!"

As he spoke, I suddenly felt my pussy start to spasm around his thickness. God, I was coming—coming harder than I ever had in my life!

"Oh...*Ohhhh!*" I gasped, bucking my hips helplessly as the pleasure rushed over me in waves. I could feel my inner walls contracting, squeezing his thick cock—almost milking it, as though I was begging him to fill me with his cream.

I knew Tark could feel it too because he suddenly thrust deep inside me and held still with his hands gripped tight around my hips.

"Gods, Babygirl, I can feel you coming all around me!" he groaned. "Your sweet little pussy and ass are milking me! It's like you're begging me to breed you!"

"I am!" I moaned. "Oh God, Daddy—please come in me!"

I didn't have to ask him again. Before I knew it, something hot and wet was spurting deep inside me, making me moan even more.

The sensation of him filling me with his cream—with his seed—was almost more than I could stand. I don't know if there was more magic involved, but I *do* know an even more intense orgasm that shot through my whole body and made me moan his name.

"Tark...*Tark!*"

I don't know how long the orgasm lasted, but I felt something happening as I came. It was almost like something was growing between me and Tark. Something that had been planted earlier—maybe even the first time we met. Something that had been strengthened when he first tasted me and made me come and was now fully grown. It seemed to twine around me like an invisible golden vine and I felt it twining around Tark at the same time.

"Gods, Babygirl—I can feel us coming together," he groaned. "You're mine now—you'll always be mine! And I'll always be yours."

"Always!" I moaned. "Oh God, Daddy—*always.*"

And I knew we would never be parted again, now that I was...
Loved by the Orc.

Author's Note — *Here is where you go back to Chapter 20 (Page 114) to finish reading the book. I hope you enjoyed this Bonus Daddy Section. This is an experiment so if you'd like to see more of my books written this way, please come see me on* Facebook* or Instagram† or TikTok‡ *to let me know you liked it!*
Hugs and Happy Reading!
Evangeline

---

* https://facebook.com/evangelineandersonauthorpage
† https://instagram.com/evangeline_anderson_author
‡ https://tiktok.com/@evangelineanderson

GIVE A HOT KINDRED WARRIOR TO A FRIEND!

Do you love the Kindred? Do you want to talk about wishing you could go live on the Mother Ship without your friends thinking you're crazy? Well, now it's super easy to get them into the Kindred universe.

Just share this link, **https://bookhip.com/HLNPTP**, with them to download *Claimed*, the first book in my Brides of the Kindred series for FREE.

No strings attached—I don't even want to collect their email for my newsletter. I just want you to be able to share the Kindred world with your besties and have fun doing it.

Hugs and Happy Reading!

Evangeline

SIGN UP FOR MY NEWSLETTER!

Sign up for my newsletter and you'll be the first to know when a new book comes out or I have some cool stuff to give away.

www.evangelineanderson.com/newsletter

Don't worry—I won't share your email with anyone else, I'll never spam you (way too busy writing books) and you can unsubscribe at any time.

As a thank-you gift you'll get a free copy of BONDING WITH THE BEAST delivered to your inbox right away. In the next days I'll also send you free copies of CLAIMED, book 1 in the Brides of Kindred series, and ABDUCTED, the first book in my Alien Mate Index series.

DO YOU LOVE AUDIOBOOKS?

You've read the book, now listen to the audiobook.

My Kindred series is coming to audio one book at a time.
Sign up for my audiobook newsletter below.

www.evangelineanderson.com/audio-newsletter

Besides notifications about new audio releases you may also get an email if I'm running a contest with an audio-book prize. Otherwise I will leave you alone. :).

BECOME A VIP!

The Aliens & Alphas Bookstore offers you exclusive (pre-)releases, special box sets, and reissues of old favorites that you can't find anywhere else.

www.shop.evangelineanderson.com

Sign up for the Aliens & Alphas VIP list to never miss a release, get exclusive sneak peeks, discounts and so much more.

www.shop.evangelineanderson.com/vip-list

ALSO BY EVANGELINE ANDERSON

Below you'll find a list of available and upcoming titles. But depending on when you read this list, new books will have come out by then that are not listed here. Make sure to check my website, www.evangelineanderson.com, for the latest releases and better yet, sign up for my newsletter (evangelineanderson.com/newsletter) to never miss a new book again.

Brides of the Kindred series

(Sci-Fi / Action-Adventure Romance)

CLAIMED

HUNTED

SOUGHT

FOUND

REVEALED

PURSUED

EXILED

SHADOWED

CHAINED

DIVIDED

DEVOURED

ENHANCED

CURSED

ENSLAVED

TARGETED

FORGOTTEN

SWITCHED

UNCHARTED

UNBOUND

SURRENDERED

VANISHED

IMPRISONED

TWISTED

DECEIVED

STOLEN

COMMITTED

PUNISHED

PIERCED

TRAPPED

RESCUED

UNWRAPPED

BRIDES OF THE KINDRED VOLUME ONE

Contains *Claimed, Hunted, Sought* and *Found*

BRIDES OF THE KINDRED VOLUME TWO

Contains *Revealed, Pursued* and *Exiled*

BRIDES OF THE KINDRED VOLUME THREE

Contains *Shadowed, Chained* and *Divided*

BRIDES OF THE KINDRED VOLUME FOUR

Contains *Devoured, Enhanced* and *Cursed*

BRIDES OF THE KINDRED VOLUME FIVE

Contains *Enslaved, Targeted* and *Forgotten*

BRIDES OF THE KINDRED VOLUME SIX

Contains *Switched, Uncharted* and *Unbound*

BRIDES OF THE KINDRED VOLUME SEVEN

Contains *Surrendered, Vanished,* and *Imprisoned*

BRIDES OF THE KINDRED VOLUME EIGHT

Contains *Twisted, Deceived,* and *Stolen*

Also, all Kindred novels are on their way to Audio, join my Audiobook Newsletter (www.evangelineanderson.com/audio-newsletter) to be notified when they come out.

Kindred Tales

The Kindred Tales are side stories in the Brides of the Kindred series which stand alone outside the main story arc.

These can be read as STAND ALONE novels.

MASTERING THE MISTRESS

BONDING WITH THE BEAST

SEEING WITH THE HEART

FREEING THE PRISONER

HEALING THE BROKEN *(a Kindred Christmas novel)*

TAMING THE GIANT

BRIDGING THE DISTANCE

LOVING A STRANGER

FINDING THE JEWEL

BONDED BY ACCIDENT

RELEASING THE DRAGON

SHARING A MATE

INSTRUCTING THE NOVICE

AWAKENED BY THE GIANT

HITTING THE TARGET

HANDLING THE HYBRID

TRAPPED IN TIME

TIME TO HEAL

PAIRING WITH THE PROTECTOR

FALLING FOR KINDRED CLAUS

GUARDING THE GODDESS

STEALING HER HEART

TAMING TWO WARRIORS

THE KINDRED WARRIOR'S CAPTIVE BRIDE

DARK AND LIGHT

PROTECTING HIS MISTRESS

UNLEASHED BY THE DEFENDER

SUBMITTING TO THE SHADOW

SECRET SANTA SURPRISE

THE PRIESTESS AND THE THIEF

PLAYING THEIR PARTS

RAISED TO KILL

HEALING HER PATIENT

DELIVERED BY THE DEFENDER

ACCIDENTAL ACQUISITION

BURNING FOR LOVE

HIDDEN RAGE

ENTICED BY THE SATYR

SAVED BY THE BEAST

LOVED BY THE LION

BONDED BY TWO

TAMING THE TIGER

DRAGON IN THE DARK

GUARDED BY THE HYBRID

QUEEN OF THEIR COLONY

FINDING HIS GODDESS

FAKING IT WITH THE HYBRID

TIED TO THE WULVEN

SHARED BY THE MONSTRUM

LOST ON OBLIVION

WICKED AND WILD

DAE'MONS AND DOMS

POSING FOR THEIR PLEASURE

GUIDED BY THE GIANT

CHOSEN BY THE CHIMERA

SHADOWED PAST

DARKEST DESIRE

TO QUENCH HER THIRST

KINDRED TALES VOLUME 1

Contains *Mastering the Mistress, Bonding with the Beast* and *Seeing with the Heart*

KINDRED TALES VOLUME 2

Contains *Freeing the Prisoner, Healing the Broken* and *Taming the Giant*

KINDRED TALES VOLUME 3

Contains *Bridging the Distance, Loving a Stranger* and *Finding the Jewel*

KINDRED TALES VOLUME 4

Contains *Bonded by Accident, Releasing the Dragon,* and *Sharing a Mate*

KINDRED TALES VOLUME 5

Contains *Instructing the Novice, Awakened by the Giant,* and *Hitting the Target*

KINDRED TALES VOLUME 6

Contains *Handling the Hybrid, Trapped in Time,* and *Time to Heal*

KINDRED TALES VOLUME 7

Contains *Pairing with the Protector, Falling for Kindred Claus,* and *Guarding the Goddess*

Kindred Tales Spicy Shorts

(Sci-Fi / Action-Adventure Romance)

These books are all stand alone novellas set in my Kindred Tales universe and can be read in any order.

TRAPPED IN THE CHRISTMAS CABIN

KIDNAPPED FROM THE PARADISE RESORT

Kindle Birthright series

(Sci-Fi / Action-Adventure Romance)

The Children of the Kindred series

UNBONDABLE

The Brutal Universe

(Sci-Fi Alien Mafia Romance)

CRUEL UNION

SAVAGE UNION

Hidden Hollow series

(Spicy Monster Romance)

SWORN TO THE ORC

DREAMING OF THE DEMON

GUARDED BY THE GARGOYLE

LOVED BY THE ORC

Born to Darkness series

(Paranormal / Action-Adventure Romance)

CRIMSON DEBT

SCARLET HEAT

RUBY SHADOWS

CARDINAL SINS (coming soon)

DESSERT (short novella following *Scarlet Heat*)

BORN TO DARKNESS BOX SET

Contains *Crimson Debt*, *Scarlet Heat*, and *Ruby Shadows* all in one volume

---

Alien Mate Index series

(Sci-Fi / Action-Adventure Romance)

ABDUCTED

PROTECTED

DESCENDED

SEVERED

THE OVERLORD'S PET

THE BARON'S BRIDE

ALIEN MATE INDEX VOLUME ONE

Contains *Abducted*, *Protected*, *Descended* and *Severed* all in one volume

All *Alien Mate* novels are now available in PRINT.

The Cougarville series

(Paranormal / Action-Adventure Romance)

(Older Woman / Younger Man)

BUCK NAKED

COUGAR BAIT

STONE COLD FOX

BIG, BAD WOLF

The CyBRG Files with Mina Carter

(Sci-Fi / Action-Adventure Romance)

UNIT 77: BROKEN

UNIT 78: RESCUED

The Institute series

(Daddy-Dom / Age Play Romance)
THE INSTITUTE: DADDY ISSUES
THE INSTITUTE: MISHKA'S SPANKING

The Swann Sister Chronicles
(Contemporary Fairy / Funny / Fantasy Romance)
WISHFUL THINKING
BE CAREFUL WHAT YOU WISH FOR

Nocturne Academy
(Young Adult Paranormal/Action-Adventure/Romance)
LOCK AND KEY
FANG AND CLAW
STONE AND SECRET

Detectives Valenti and O'Brian
(1980s M/M Romance)
THE ASSIGNMENT
I'LL BE HOT FOR CHRISTMAS
FIREWORKS
THE ASSIGNMENT: HEART AND SOUL

Forbidden Omegaverse Series

(Paranormal Romance
Step-Brother / Foster Brother Romance)
HIS OMEGA'S KEEPER
THE BRAND THAT BINDS
HEAT CYCLE
SINS OF THE FLESH
FORBIDDEN DESIRE

The Shadow Fae
(Dark Fantasy Romance)
THE THRONE OF SHADOWS
THE QUEEN OF MIDNIGHT

Compendiums and Box Sets
ALIEN MATE INDEX VOLUME ONE
Contains *Abducted*, *Protected*, *Descended* and *Severed* all in one volume
BORN TO DARKNESS BOX SET
Contains *Crimson Debt*, *Scarlet Heat*, and *Ruby Shadows* all in one volume
BRIDES OF THE KINDRED VOLUME ONE
Contains *Claimed*, *Hunted*, *Sought* and *Found*
BRIDES OF THE KINDRED VOLUME TWO
Contains *Revealed*, *Pursued* and *Exiled*
BRIDES OF THE KINDRED VOLUME THREE
Contains *Shadowed*, *Chained* and *Divided*
BRIDES OF THE KINDRED VOLUME FOUR

Contains *Devoured, Enhanced* and *Cursed*

BRIDES OF THE KINDRED VOLUME FIVE

Contains *Enslaved, Targeted* and *Forgotten*

BRIDES OF THE KINDRED VOLUME SIX

Contains *Switched, Uncharted* and *Unbound*

BRIDES OF THE KINDRED VOLUME SEVEN

Contains *Surrendered, Vanished,* and *Imprisoned*

BRIDES OF THE KINDRED VOLUME EIGHT

Contains *Twisted, Deceived,* and *Stolen*

HAVE YOURSELF A SEXY LITTLE CHRISTMAS

Contains *Kidnapped for Christmas, Cougar Christmas* and *Season's Spankings*

KINDRED TALES VOLUME 1

Contains *Mastering the Mistress, Bonding with the Beast* and *Seeing with the Heart*

KINDRED TALES VOLUME 2

Contains *Freeing the Prisoner, Healing the Broken* and *Taming the Giant*

KINDRED TALES VOLUME 3

Contains *Bridging the Distance, Loving a Stranger* and *Finding the Jewel*

KINDRED TALES VOLUME 4

Contains *Bonded by Accident, Releasing the Dragon,* and *Sharing a Mate*

KINDRED TALES VOLUME 5

Contains *Instructing the Novice, Awakened by the Giant,* and *Hitting the Target*

KINDRED TALES VOLUME 6

Contains *Handling the Hybrid, Trapped in Time,* and *Time to Heal*

KINDRED TALES VOLUME 7

Contains *Pairing with the Protector, Falling for Kindred Claus,* and *Guarding the Goddess*

NAUGHTY TALES: THE COLLECTION— Volume One

Contains *Putting on a Show, Willing Submission, The Institute: Daddy Issues, The Institute: Mishka's Spanking, Confessions of a Lingerie Model, Sin Eater, Speeding Ticket, Stress Relief* and *When Mr. Black Comes Home.*

ONE HOT HALLOWEEN

Contains *Red and the Wolf, Gypsy Moon* and *Taming the Beast*

ONE HOT HALLOWEEN Vol.2

Contains *The Covenant, Secret Thirst,* and *Kristen's Addiction* + BONUS: *Madeline's Mates*

Stand Alone Titles

(Sci-Fi OR Paranormal Action-Adventure Romance)

ANYONE U WANT

BEST KEPT SECRETS (Step-Brother romance)

BLIND DATE WITH A VAMPIRE

BLOOD KISS

BROKEN BOUNDARIES (M/M romance)

CEREMONY OF THREE

COMPANION 3000

DEAL WITH THE DEVIL

DEFILED

EYES LIKE A WOLF (Foster Brother romance)

FOREVER BROKEN (M/M romance)

GYPSY MOON

HUNGER MOON RISING

MADELINE'S MATES

MARKED

OUTCAST

PLANET X

PLEASURE PLANET

PLEDGE SLAVE (M/M romance)

PUNISHING TABITHA

PURITY

RED AND THE WOLF

SECRET THIRST

SEX WITH STRANGERS

SHADOW DREAMS

SLAVE BOY (M/M romance)

STRESS RELIEF

SWEET DREAMS

TAMING THE BEAST

TANDEM UNIT

THE BARGAIN

THE COVENANT

THE LAST BITE (M/M romance)

THE LAST MAN ON EARTH

THE LOST BOOKS (M/M romance)

THE PLEASURE PALACE

THE SACRIFICE

'TIL KINGDOM COME (M/M romance)

Stand Alone Titles

(Contemporay Romance)

A SPANKING FOR VALENTINE (BDSM)

BOUND AND DETERMINED, anthology with Lena Matthews, includes *The Punishment of Nicollett*

COUGAR CHRISTMAS (Older Woman / Younger Man)

DANGEROUS CRAVINGS (BDSM)

DIRTY GIRL

FULL EXPOSURE (with Lena Matthews)

KIDNAPPED FOR CHRISTMAS (BDSM)

MASKS (BDSM)

MORE THAN FRIENDS (BDSM)

PICTURE PERFECT (Step-Brother romance)

STR8TE BOYS (M/M romance)

Naughty Tales

(Short Reads to Get You Hot and Bothered)

CONFESSIONS OF A LINGERIE MODEL

PUTTING ON A SHOW (Step-Brother romance)

SIN EATER

SPEEDING TICKET

THE SWITCH (An erotic interlude with the characters of DANGEROUS CRAVINGS)

SEASON'S SPANKINGS

WHEN MR. BLACK COMES HOME

WILLING SUBMISSION

NAUGHTY TALES: THE COLLECTION— Volume One

Contains *Putting on a Show, Willing Submission, The Institute: Daddy Issues, The Institute: Mishka's Spanking, Confessions of a Lingerie Model, Sin Eater, Speeding Ticket, Stress Relief* and *When Mr. Black Comes Home.*

YA Novels

THE ACADEMY

ABOUT THE AUTHOR

Evangeline Anderson is the *New York Times* and *USA Today* bestselling author of the *Brides of the Kindred*, *Alien Mate Index*, *Cougarville*, and *Born to Darkness* series. She lives in Florida with a husband, a son, and the voices in her head. (Mostly characters who won't shut up.) She has been writing sci-fi and paranormal romance for years and she welcomes reader comments and suggestions at **www.evangelineanderson.com**.

Or, to be the first to find out about new books, join her newsletter: **www.evangelineanderson.com/newsletter**

For updates on Young Adult releases only sign up here instead: **www.evangelineanderson.com/young-adult-newsletter**

She's also got a mailing list for updates on audio books: **www.evangelineanderson.com/audio-newsletter**

- facebook.com/evangelineandersonauthorpage
- x.com/EvangelineA
- instagram.com/evangeline_anderson_author
- pinterest.com/vangiekitty
- goodreads.com/evangelineanderson
- bookbub.com/authors/evangeline-anderson
- tiktok.com/@evangelineanderson

Made in United States
Troutdale, OR
05/03/2025